# Drop Dead

"Dr. Darity? Do you usually leave the windows open in the middle of fall?"

"What?"

I pointed at the second floor of the house, where a pair of pink curtains were flapping out of an open window.

"That's Destiny's room!"

Dr. Darity pulled a set of keys from his pocket and raced to the front door of the house. He threw the door open and Killer ran in, leaping up the stairs. Toward the room with the open window.

When we got to the top of the stairs, the door was closed. Dr. Darity flung it open.

"No!" he yelled, stopped by the scene in front of him.

Her eyes closed, Destiny's body lay sprawled on the floor!

# THE HARDY BOYS

Undercover Brothers®

**Available from Simon & Schuster**

# THE HARDY BOYS

Undercover Brothers®

# FRANKLIN W. DIXON

## #32 Private Killer

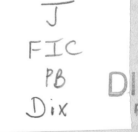

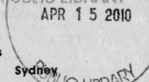
**Aladdin Paperbacks**
**New York   London   Toronto   Sydney**

ALADDIN

An imprint of Simon & Schuster Children's Publishing Division
1230 Avenue of the Americas, New York, NY 10020
First Aladdin paperback edition January 2010
Text copyright © 2010 by Simon & Schuster, Inc.
All rights reserved, including the right of reproduction in whole or in part in any form.
ALADDIN is a trademark of Simon & Schuster, Inc., and related logo is a registered trademark of Simon & Schuster, Inc. THE HARDY BOYS and THE HARDY BOYS MYSTERY STORIES are registered trademarks of Simon & Schuster, Inc.
For information about special discounts for bulk purchases, please contact Simon & Schuster Special Sales at 1-866-506-1949 or business @simonandschuster.com.
The Simon & Schuster Speakers Bureau can bring authors to your live event. For more information or to book an event contact the Simon & Schuster Speakers Bureau at 1-866-248-3049 or visit our website at www .simonspeakers.com.
Designed by Sammy Yuen Jr.
The text of this book was set in Aldine 401 BT.
Manufactured in the United States of America
1109 OFF
10 9 8 7 6 5 4 3 2 1
Library of Congress Control Number 2009932238
ISBN 978-1-4169-8697-3
ISBN 978-1-4169-9856-3 (eBook)

# TABLE OF CONTENTS

# The Writing on the Wall

*J**ust once,*** I thought as I stared at the two buckets full of red liquid, *couldn't it be cherry cough syrup?*

Killer, the former police dog turned school mascot, seemed to know exactly what it was. He growled low and deep at the buckets. I stepped up and held up my finger, which I'd just dipped into the fluid to confirm my suspicion.

My stomach churned. "Looks like we've got another mystery on our hands."

*"Blood?"* my brother Frank asked.

Everyone around me—except for Frank—immediately drew back.

"What kind of sick person would do something like that?" asked Mr. Marks. His face was pale, and he sounded genuinely disgusted, which was almost funny considering that his son Ellery had just been found responsible for the death of one student and the serious wounding of another. In fact, if I had to take a guess as to "what kind of sick person" would do something like this, I'd pretty much lay my money on Ellery. Speaking of which . . .

"Where's Ellery?"

The adults looked around in confusion. Could Ellery have taken this opportunity to make a run for it? Frank nodded at me and rushed outside to look for him.

"He's here," Frank yelled a second later. I was about to ask what he was doing out there, when an unmistakable sound echoed around the walls of the little cabin.

*BLUGH—BLUGH—BLEAAARGH!*

Sounded like Ellery, for all his murderous ways, couldn't handle the sight of blood. I wasn't that surprised really. He seemed pretty unstable—he'd killed someone just to get out of having to join the fraternity his father had been in! Talk about over-reacting. This didn't seem like him. Buckets of blood were too cold and calculating.

It was pretty clear Ellery knew nothing about the blood. And from his reaction, it didn't look likehis father did either. So what were two buckets of blood doing in an abandoned hut in the middle of nowhere on the grounds of the exclusive Willis Firth Academy? Whose blood was it? Something told me that this case wasn't as over as we'd thought it was. Seems like Ellery wasn't the only one making trouble around here.

"Whose hut is this, anyway?" I asked Dr. Darity.

He shrugged. "I didn't even know this existed," he said. "I'll look into it, but there have been a lot of renovations done to the grounds over the years. Who knows when it was built?"

"Well, until we have more information, we need to have security watching this place. No one gets in or out."

"I think I can help with that," said Mr. Marks. "I can leave behind one of my private security detail. Just until the school can hire security of their own, of course."

"Thank you, but—"

Mr. Marks cut Dr. Darity off. "No need to thank me. But perhaps some of the more . . . *sordid* details of the events of the past few hours could be kept quiet?"

Guess he didn't want the whole world knowing his son had gone off the deep end. I couldn't blame him for that.

"Of course the school will be discrete, Mr.—"

"Good," Mr. Marks said. "I will be removing Ellery from the school immediately. Your organization—what's it called again? ALAC? ALAS?"

"ATAC," I said. I'd forgotten that Mr. Marks and Ellery knew all about our real reason for being at the school. That made me nervous; I wondered who else knew.

"Right. ATAC has suggested a place where Ellery might be taken care of until he is recovered from this illness. He and I will be heading there by private jet tomorrow. You may keep my bodyguard for as long as necessary. Oh, and Dr. Darity—I assume that none of this unpleasantness will interfere with the Annual Firth-Blair Benevolence Weekend next week. Because as the head of the alumni association, I can assure you, people would be upset. Everyone wants the big game to go on."

With that, he turned and left. I heard him grab Ellery on the way out. Frank came back in. Dr. Darity had his head in his hands.

"What am I going to tell the students?" he mumbled. "What am I going to tell the parents? This is a disaster."

"You can't mention this to anyone," said Frank. "Until we figure out more about whose blood this is, this could cause a panic—which is exactly what this person seems to want. Someone is out to get this school."

"Yeah," I added. "And we're out to get them first." I wanted to ask him more about this weekend thing and the upcoming game. I'd heard students talking about it since we'd arrived on campus, and it seemed like a big deal. But now wasn't the time.

Frank pulled out a square black case from his back pocket, about the size of an MP3 player. He flipped it open. One side was lined with all sorts of things: tiny bottles, tweezers, eye droppers, etc. The other side was a tiny computer we'd nicknamed JuDGE: Junior Data Gathering Equipment. It was wirelessly connected to a giant mainframe computer at ATAC headquarters. Any evidence placed within the computer's main compartment would be remotely analyzed within a few hours.

Frank pulled on a pair of rubber gloves and carefully drew up a sample of blood from one of the buckets. He placed a single drop inside the open compartment in JuDGE's center, then closed the tiny plastic window. Instantly, the computer came to life and began transmitting information home. Frank folded it shut and put it back inside his pocket.

"There," he said. "It should be able to tell us where it came from pretty quickly. And if there's a match for the source in our database, we might even get some specific information by morning."

"You boys don't think it's—it couldn't be—I mean, it's not . . . *human*, is it?" asked Dr. Darity.

Frank and I exchanged a look.

"That much blood? There's no way," I told Dr. Darity. "Besides, no one else has been reported injured, right?"

Dr. Darity nodded.

"We'd have heard about it by now if it came from a student. This is probably just a prank. I bet someone bought it from a butcher shop or something." *I hope,* I added silently.

Just then a big beefy guy in a bad gray suit peeked in the door. He was built like a man-mountain.

"Mr. Marks sent me," he rumbled, his voice like an avalanche. "Said to keep people out."

Dr. Darity nodded. "Yes, thank you."

Frank and I escorted Dr. Darity out of the hut, with Killer walking along beside us. "Let's get some sleep," I said. "Hopefully, by the morning, ATAC will have all the information we need."

JuDGE beeped. It had finished its preliminary analysis. Frank pulled it out of his pocket.

The look on his face said everything.

"It's human."

The best part about this mission was that I wasn't posing as a student. So while Frank had to worry about classes and tests, all I had to do was take care of Killer. Even if the dog didn't love me the way he did his old handler, Hunt Hunter, he was too well trained to be much of a problem. In fact, the only bad part was that Killer was totally a morning dog. He liked his first walk right after dawn! It was almost as bad as having to get up for school. On the plus side, we were hoping to get information from ATAC about the source of the blood this morning, so I'd have to be up anyway.

Half-awake, I dragged myself over to the cafeteria. After last night, I was going to need some serious sugar to wake me up enough to be able to handle Killer. I grabbed a couple of donuts and a big plate of Frosted Kitten-Os. The cafeteria served both students and staff, but the only people awake this early were some of the cleaning crew. They had one table near the back, and there was a steady hum of conversation as I approached. Word must have been going around about the events of last night.

"Have you heard?"

That was the first thing someone said to me when I sat down. I played dumb, figuring I'd get a chance to see what information had leaked.

"Heard about what?"

Erik Hudson, one of the cleaning crew members I'd met a few times before, pulled his chair closer to mine. He was a nice guy, and he loved his gossip. At places like Firth Academy, the cleaning crew always had the best gossip, since the students rarely ever noticed they existed. And by the excited expression on his face, Erik definitely had some good gossip today.

"Dude! Someone trashed the soccer team's locker room!"

My ears perked up. This wasn't what I was expecting. "Trashed it how?"

"That's the sick part! There was blood all over the room. Some psycho had painted the words 'GET OUT' in blood on the walls."

*So that's what the blood was from!* I thought. But out loud I simply said "Gross."

"You're telling me," said Erik. "I was the one who had to clean it up. I don't think I'll ever get that smell out of my nose."

"I wonder why anyone would do that?" I said, hoping to keep Erik talking.

"I don't know. But whoever did it sure doesn't like Lee Jenkins."

"What do you mean?"

"They destroyed his locker. Ripped the hinges off, poured blood on the stuff inside it. Really messed with him."

*Interesting.* Lee Jenkins was a junior, a star soccer player, a new Gamma Theta Theta pledge, and a straight-A student who also happened to be one of the few kids at the school whose family wasn't megarich. He was the poster boy for Dr. Darity's scholarship program, which let students from poor backgrounds get some of the incredible opportunities that an education at the Firth Academy afforded the rich kids who made up most of the student body.

I needed to talk with Frank about all of this. I shoveled the last of my Frosted Kitten-Os into my mouth and grabbed another donut on my way out the door.

Frank met me back outside of Killer's kennel. Frank, like Killer, was a morning person, and he seemed bright and chipper as he came running toward us. Killer pulled on the leash and leaped up on him as soon as he got near. Killer loved Frank.

"Have you heard?" I asked.

"Heard what?" Frank replied.

"The blood—it's all over the school!"

"It is?" He looked around, checking for anyone who might be able to overhear us talking. "Where?"

"Word about the blood was all over the school this morning. All the servers in the dining hall were talking about it. Apparently someone used it to trash the boys' locker room. They wrote 'GET OUT' in big letters across the room. And get this—whoever did it also trashed Lee's locker specifically."

"Seems like someone doesn't want Lee around," Frank said.

I remembered that this wasn't the first time Lee had been messed with while we were here. Someone had also mysteriously hacked in to the computer and changed his grades.

"Yeah, but who? Whoever did this couldn't have been with us last night."

"Right. So that knocks out Ellery and his father."

"Spencer too." Spencer was the president of Gamma Theta Theta. He seemed like an all-around good guy, but a lot of the stuff that had gone wrong had happened while he was around, so we hadn't ruled him out as a suspect quite yet.

I let Killer off his leash as we approached the woods surrounding campus. He bounded out into the woods, looking like a playful puppy. A playful, one hundred pound, police-trained puppy.

"Well," said Frank after a minute. "Patton seemed pretty pissed that they were going to let Lee into Gamma Theta Theta."

Patton Gage was another junior pledging GTT, and he seemed desperate to get in. He was pretty jealous of all the other pledges—including Lee.

"He was injured last night in Ellery's prank, but I didn't see him before we got to the GTT house," I said. He'd ended up with some pretty bad burns from some acid, but the ambulance crew had assured us he would be all right.

"Me either," said Frank. "He would have had more than enough time to trash the locker room and hide the blood before heading over to GTT."

I hated to say it, but there was one other suspect we needed to consider.

"What about Destiny?" I asked. Destiny Darity was the daughter of Dr. Darity, the school's head-master, and she was the only female student at Willis Firth Academy. She had a reputation for being a troublemaker, and we'd seen her slap Lee during an argument just a few days earlier. If anyone had the temper to pull off a stunt like this, it was Destiny.

"Since you have class with Patton, why don't you try to talk to him when he gets back from the hospital?" I suggested.

Frank grinned. "Right. And that way you can talk to Destiny, eh?"

Did I mention that Destiny was seriously cute? And that she seemed to have a crush on me? All right, most of her crush seemed to be an act designed to make her dad angry, but still. I couldn't help but be flattered. I nodded.

"Any excuse to get close to the girl." Frank laughed.

We were approaching the athletics department now. I could hear the soccer team warming up down below. They were the star of the Firth Academy sports teams. Rumor had it they might go all-state this year. Aside from Lee, the surprise star of the team was Destiny Darity. She'd been the goalie on the girls' soccer team at her old school, and since Firth Academy required that all students participate in at least one team activity, she'd tried out for the soccer team here. Everyone—with the exception of Destiny herself—was shocked when she'd made the varsity team.

"What are they doing up so early?" I asked Frank. "I thought they practiced after classes?"

"There's that big game coming up, remember? It's a grudge match with another private school, their longtime rivals. Apparently, this year is their big chance to win back the championship."

We stopped and watched them practice. After a minute, something occurred to me. "Hey—do you see Destiny down there?"

"No . . . where is she?"

The practice was breaking up now, and there was no sign of Destiny anywhere.

"I've got a bad feeling about this," I said.

"Me too. Let's go check in with Dr. Darity."

I called Killer back and put him on his leash. We set off at a quick walk across campus. By the time we found our way to Dr. Darity's office, everyone was up and talking about the events of last night.

"Hey Dr. D.," said Frank as we walked into his office.

"Hi Frank. Joe. I've been so caught up in trying to get the details settled for the Benevolence Weekend next Saturday, I haven't had a chance to find out anything more about that hut in the woods yet. Or the Brothers of Erebus."

The Brothers of Erebus was some sort of secret society within the Gamma Theta Theta fraternity, and they had been the group that Ellery had really been trying to get out of. We still didn't really know who they were or what they did. They put the "secret" in secret society. Dr. Darity looked like he hadn't slept in a year. There were big black bags under his eyes, and his clothes were all wrinkled.

"Have you seen Destiny this morning? She wasn't at soccer practice," I said.

"No," said Dr. Darity. "I wasn't going to mention it, but . . . she has a habit of disappearing. I've tried everything to get her to tell me when she leaves. I've bought cell phones, calling cards. But I think she enjoys making me worry. She's been gone since yesterday afternoon."

Frank and I exchanged a look. This was definitely not good.

"I'm sure she's all right though," said Dr. Darity.

The way he said it, he didn't sound sure at all.

I tried to reassure him.

"She's probably fine. Still, we should find her. Do you have any idea where she might be?"

Dr. Darity opened his mouth, but Frank's phone rang before he could say anything.

"Yes?" said Frank as he answered the phone. His face turned pale. "Right. Yes, we're with him now. Okay."

"Dr. Darity?" Frank said. "That was ATAC. They've identified the blood—it's Destiny's."

FRANK

# 2

## Bad Blood

"That's not possible!" Dr. Darity bellowed. "It has to be some sort of mistake."

He surged out of his seat, ready to run out the office door and find Destiny—if the trash basket hadn't gotten in his way. Joe caught Dr. Darity before he slammed into the wall, and slowly lowered him to the ground.

"Listen to me," I said. "Panicking isn't going to help Destiny. Have you tried calling her?" From the amount of blood we'd seen in those buckets, I wasn't sure anything could help Destiny at this point, but we needed Dr. Darity to be able to cooperate with us, which meant giving him hope.

He pulled out his cell phone and dialed Destiny's

number. His hands, I noticed, were oddly still for someone who just found out his daughter was missing a couple of buckets of blood.

"Yo!" Destiny's voice echoed loudly from the receiver.

"Destiny!" Dr. Darity yelled. I breathed a sigh of relief. She was still alive.

"You've reached Destiny's cell. Leave me a message. I'll call you back—if I feel like it. LATERS!"

*Well,* I thought, *there goes that hope.*

Dr. Darity spoke evenly into the phone. "Destiny, you have to call me. Do you hear me? Call me the second you get this message!"

Joe and I exchanged a look. Not that I knew what it was like to be a father. But if I'd just found buckets of my own daughter's blood, I'd be a mess. Darity almost seemed . . . more angry than upset for his daughter's well-being.

"Dr. Darity? Do you have anything of Destiny's here in the office? Killer's been police trained; I'm sure with something of hers to smell, he could find her—"

I cut Joe off before he could say the word "body."

"Killer could find Destiny," I said, giving Joe a dirty look. He mouthed the word *sorry*.

"Her scarf is over there." Dr. Darity pointed

to the back of the office door. Joe brought Killer over.

"Does Destiny have any enemies, Dr. Darity? Anyone who might want to hurt her?"

"I—I—Well, Destiny is a misunderstood girl. You have to understand. Her mother died and—"

"Dr. Darity, please. We don't have a lot of time. Just tell me. Had she made anyone angry?"

Dr. Darity sighed and rubbed his eyes. Finally, after a minute, he spoke.

"Who hasn't she made angry? She's been kicked out of every school she's ever attended. She's smart, but she picks fights and doesn't try hard at anything—except for soccer. At her last school, the Hallie Blair School, Destiny had a long-standing rivalry with this girl Lydia. I'm sad to say that she did some pretty mean things. It sounds like both of the girls did. But in the end, Destiny shaved the poor girl's head because she thought it was her fault they'd lost a game. That was the last straw, and the Blair School expelled her after that."

*The Blair School? Where had I heard that name before?* I didn't have time to think about it right now, but I filed it away in my brain for later.

"What about here? Is there anyone at Firth who might have a grudge against her?"

"She's had a hard time here. A lot of the school

didn't want her here—the old boys network, you know?—but the trustees were happy with the job I'd done since I started at Firth, and, with some serious coaxing, they made an exception. She didn't have anywhere else to go, and she only has one year of high school left to finish. I thought people would get over it, but ever since she joined the soccer team, it's been a thousand times worse. Her tires have been slashed. Prank calls. Someone toilet papered our house. Every week something new happens."

"Dr. Darity, all due respect but . . . this sounds pretty serious," I said. "Why didn't you tell us any of this earlier?"

Dr. Darity shrugged, looking baffled and defeated. "Honestly, I didn't see any connection. Before now, it didn't seem to have been related in any way to everything else. But now with this prank . . ."

*Prank?!* I thought. That amount of blood added up to one of two possible conclusions: either Destiny was dead or dying. Prank isn't the word I would have used to describe what basically amounted to murder. Something was not right here, and Joe and I both knew it.

Joe tossed me a nod and held Destiny's scarf out for Killer to sniff. "Well, let's see where it takes us."

"Come on boy," Joe said to Killer, leading him out the door. "Find Destiny."

Killer whined and snuffled, digging his nose deep in the scarf. Outside, he perked his head up. He started pulling on the leash.

"Come on." I pulled Dr. Darity to his feet. The fact that Killer had found a trail seemed to bring him back to himself. With Killer leading the way, we ran from the administration building back toward the main quad of the school.

All around, students were enjoying their afternoon. We barged through a group of guys grilling burgers and interrupted a Frisbee game. Killer patrolled back and forth across the grass, looking for the freshest, most recent scent. Finally he found something. His ears perked up and he bounded forward, pulling Joe behind him. Dr. Darity and I ran to keep up.

Finally Killer came to a stop—right outside of Darity's house.

"Come on Killer, come on!" Joe tried to coax Killer away from the house and back on Destiny's trail, but Killed wouldn't move.

"Could he have lost her scent?" asked Dr. Darity.

I looked over at the Darity house. At first glance, the blue house looked cozy and quiet. But then I realized there was something strange.

"Dr. Darity? Do you usually leave the windows open in the middle of fall?"

"What?"

I pointed at the second floor of the house, where a pair of pink curtains were flapping out of an open window.

"That's Destiny's room!"

Dr. Darity pulled a set of keys from his pocket and raced to the front door of the house. He threw the door open and Killer ran in, leaping up the stairs. Toward the room with the open window.

When we got to the top of the stairs, the door was closed. Dr. Darity flung it open.

"No!" he yelled, stopped by the scene in front of him.

Her eyes closed, Destiny's body lay sprawled on the floor!

## The Living Dead

"Destiny!" Dr. Darity's voice choked out as he looked at the body of his daughter lying on the ground. I placed a hand on Dr. Darity's arm, unsure what to say.

Suddenly Destiny's eyes flew open.

"Dad?" she said.

She pulled the headphones from her ears, and I caught a brief blast of some wailing guitars. Then she noticed Frank and me.

"Oh my God! What are you doing in my room?" She stared at me for a while.

I'd always thought that zombies could only say things like "BRAAAINS" or "HUUMANS!" Destiny, however, seemed to have kept a firm grasp on English. Also, she didn't really seem to be injured. Mostly, she just looked . . . *angry*. And boy did she look cute when she was angry!

"I know we're living in like, a police state and all, but can't I get any privacy?" She shoved a bunch of stuff under her bed, which already looked like it had about twenty closets worth of stuff pushed under it, and stomped around the room.

"Destiny! You're all right!" Dr. Darity looked like he might break out in tears at any moment. He grabbed her in a big hug.

"Uh . . . yeah? So are you?" said Destiny, as she struggled to breathe in her father's tight grasp. She "noticed Killer for the first time.

"Oh great," she said. "You brought the mutt, too. Try not to let it drool on any of my things, okay?"

Suddenly her father pushed her out to arm's length and held her there by her shoulders. "Where have you been? I have been worried sick about you all weekend! You have no idea what's been going on here."

"Daaad," said Destiny. "I just went to Boston for the night. I was stressed out, you know? I just needed to get away for the weekend. Plus, some twerp GTT pledge tried to sneak in and steal my bathing suit for like, the third time this month.

And there was this awesome Pixies cover band playing at the Rat Trap, so . . ."

"How many times have I told you that this sort of behavior is unacceptable, Destiny?" Dr. Darity had gone from "glad Destiny was alive" to "wanting to strangle her" in about two and a half seconds.

"I was going to call you, but I lost my cell phone and my keys at the concert. That's why I had to use the window to break in. I just got home like an hour ago." Destiny pointed to the open window.

Dr. Darity let out a big sigh. All of the anger seemed to flow out of him. He flopped down on Destiny's bed.

"Ow!" he said. "Destiny, you really need to clean up around here. There's so much stuff under your bed I can hardly sit on it!"

"Yeah, I know." Destiny blushed for a second. "I'm totally going to do that today. So . . . if you guys want to leave, I could, like, get to that?" She gave Frank and me a pointed look.

"You'll have lots of time to do that—since you're going to be grounded for the next two weeks. But right now, the boys and I have something we need to talk to you about."

"Right," I said. "Like how you're up and walking around when a couple of gallons of your blood are well across campus." I explained what happened last night. When I got to the part about the blood, she shot up.

"What? My supply! If they use this as an excuse to keep me out of the big game against the Blair School next weekend, I swear I'll kill someone."

Frank stopped short. "You keep a supply of your own blood on hand?"

*Why would anyone need to do that?* I thought.

But her father was nodding. "Destiny has a very rare blood type, inherited from her mother, as well as a mild case of hemophilia, inherited from me. She frequently needs transfusions, and with a rare blood type we needed to be sure her blood was stored on campus. I had a feeling it had something to do with the supply, but until we were sure . . ." His eyes welled up. "I just wanted to be sure she was okay."

Destiny rolled her eyes. "Gee, thanks, Dad. Just tell them I'm a medical freak, why don't you?"

"Hemophilia?" I asked. "That's when you don't have the stuff that makes your blood clot, right?"

"Yep," said Destiny. "I'm a bleeder. Want to see?" Destiny held out her arm and Frank backed up a step.

"Destiny, that isn't funny!" Dr. Darity was definitely irritated. "Thankfully she doesn't have as serious a case as some. But still, she needs to be careful." This was said with a pointed look in her direction.

Destiny looked around the room at all of our faces. Then she laughed.

"You thought I was dead, didn't you? That is so cute." She reached out and ruffled my hair. "Cute" wasn't quite the "hot" I was hoping for, but I'd take it. For once, the cute girl was going after me, not Frank! It was a miracle.

I smelled something strange on her arm— smoke?

Her father smelled it too.

"When did you say you got home?" Dr. Darity sounded angry again.

"An hour ago . . ."

"Right. So you weren't at the bonfire last night? The one in town that a bunch of students snuck out to?"

"Well . . . maybe I got back a little earlier from the concert than I thought, and I dropped by briefly. For like, ten seconds."

"Did I say you were grounded for two weeks? I meant four."

"Dad! That's so not fair!"

"Do you want to go for five?"

While the Daritys fought about curfews and

punishments, Frank and I quickly slipped out of the room. We pulled Killer out with us. At least that was one mystery solved—and for once, solved without a corpse at the end.

Killer pulled us over to a bush that he wanted to, uh . . . investigate. Away from the house, Frank and I finally had a chance to talk.

"It seems like Destiny is off the hook for this one," I said.

"Yeah," agreed Frank. "It seems like this was as much a prank on her as it was on Lee."

"So who has it out for both of them?"

We thought for a second. Then it came to me. "Patton! He's had it out for Lee because he thought Lee was stealing his place at GTT, and he was angry at Dr. Darity for threatening to close down the frats. He could have done the stuff with the blood before Ellery's acid-trap got him."

Frank considered for a minute. "It's possible," he said. "But if so, we won't know until he's out of the hospital in a few days. Still, we should keep him on our list of suspects."

"If it was Patton, with him in the hospital and Ellery in a mental institution, things should be pretty quiet around here from now on."

Frank nodded. "Doesn't seem too likely, does it?" he said.

"Did you notice how weird Dr. Darity was about withholding information about Destiny?" I asked Frank.

"Like that there might be a reason for buckets of her blood to be laying around the school?" he asked. "Yeah, I noticed. But what motive would he have for the rest of it?"

---

Suspect Profile

Suspect: Patton "Peachy" Gage

Hometown: Miami, Florida

Physical Description: 5'9", 155 pounds, pale skin, red hair, freckles

Occupation: Junior at Firth; GTT pledge

Suspected Of: Trashing the Firth soccer team's locker room, threatening Lee Jenkins, and harassing Destiny Darity.

Possible Motives: Trying to get Lee to drop out so he would become the number one GTT pledge; revenge on Dr. Darity for threatening to close down the frats.

He was right. Something gave me the feeling that our real culprit was still out there. Who had changed Lee's grades and nearly gotten him kicked off the team? Not Ellery. And Destiny's father had said this wasn't the first time she'd been harassed. Still, until we had something more to go on, there was nothing we could do.

"Let's finish up Killer's walk," said Frank. "I've got to get back to studying. The classes here are hard!"

The way he said hard, it sounded more like he meant "fun." That was Frank for you.

We walked out past the Darity house, back the way we had come. Soccer practice was over now, so the path to that athletics department was empty.

"Seems like all the action involves the soccer team," I said.

"Yeah," Frank agreed. "It's probably too late to join, but I wonder if there's some way I can help out."

"Water boy?"

Frank shot me a dirty look. "Very funny," he said.

I noticed that Killer was lagging behind us. *That's odd,* I thought. Usually Killer was pulling me along. That dog couldn't get enough exercise—I guess the life of a school mascot was a lot less interesting than that of a police dog. At least usually . . . recently they had been pretty similar.

"What's up with Killer?" asked Frank.

Killer was pulling back against the leash, sitting down on his haunches. His nose was in the air and he was sniffing loudly. He was also making a low growling noise and, finally, he began tugging at the leash.

*When,* I wondered, *have I seen this before?*

Then I smelled it. "Smoke!" I yelled.

"Over there!" Frank pointed dead ahead. A plume of thick, dark smoke was rising up in the distance, right above the soccer field. This wasn't some pretty chimney smoke, or even a party bonfire. This was oily black smoke in a place where nothing was supposed to be burning. That bad feeling I'd had just a moment before came back . . . with friends.

We took off at a run—or at least tried to. Killer pulled forward violently.

Frank was a few steps ahead of me when we finally crested the last hill before the soccer field. Someone had set one of the goal posts on fire. The paint and the chemically treated wood were responsible for the dark, dirty looking smoke.

Then I looked more closely. There was a body tied to the post!

FRANK

4

# Where There's Smoke . . .

Someone was tied to that goal post! And from here, it didn't look like they were moving. I started to run down to the field, and sped up when I realized Joe and Killer had surged past me.

Joe was barely keeping up with Killer. I grabbed Killer's leash from Joe.

"Grab a fire extinguisher from one of the athletics buildings," I yelled to Joe over my shoulder.

I pulled out my cell phone and quickly dialed 911.

"This is an emergency on the grounds of the Willis Firth Academy. I need an ambulance and a fire truck at the soccer field immediately." I hung up as soon as the operator confirmed they were on their way. I was almost at the goal post now. I could just make out the person beneath the spreading flames and giant smoke clouds. I hoped I wasn't too late already.

I yanked off my coat and began to beat at the flames. I pulled my sweater up over my face to block out the worst of the smoke, but it was still like sucking on a car exhaust pipe.

I didn't put out the fire, but my swinging coat fanned enough of the smoke away that I could see the person tied to the post. Or rather I could see that it *wasn't* a person!

It was a scarecrow of some kind, or a crude mannequin. It looked like it had been made out of a couple of pieces of old two-by-fours nailed together. No wonder it was burning so well.

Even though it had been mostly destroyed by the fire already, it wasn't hard to make out who it was supposed to be. If the half-melted black wig on its head wasn't enough of a clue, someone had dressed it in a long black skirt and other women's clothes. I wouldn't be surprised if those were some of the stolen items Destiny had been complaining about earlier. Of course, they'd capped it all off with a sign that read RIP: DESTINY DARITY, just in case we hadn't gotten the hint already.

I heard footsteps running behind me. I turned

and saw Joe barreling down the hill with a fire extinguisher in his arms. In the distance I could already hear the sirens of the town's ambulance coming this way. By the time Joe got to the goal post, though, the fire had already started to die down.

"What the?" he said, as he got close enough to see that the "person" was really just a simple stick figure.

I pointed to the sign at the top of the post.

"Looks like Destiny has made someone really angry."

I nodded. That was the understatement of the year. "Maybe you should go get Killer out of here. Who knows what he'll get up to by himself. And besides, I don't think people should see us together at the scene of something like this. Ellery already knew about ATAC. Who knows what he's hinted at to other people."

Joe nodded. "Yeah, the less we're seen together the better, I think."

He took off at a run. I still had a minute or two before the emergency workers showed up, so I tried to do a quick survey of the area. I had no doubt that pretty much all of the evidence would have been destroyed by the fire, but maybe our arsonist was careless.

The field was pretty torn up by constant practicing—the soccer team had been gearing up for the big game against the Blair School for a month now. They were out here nearly every day, and sometimes twice a day. There would be no footprints to be found.

*Wait,* I thought. *The big game everyone's talking about—that's against the Blair School. And Dr. Darity said that was Destiny's old school. Interesting.*

It wasn't a lead yet, but I filed the information away for later. I'd have to find out more about the whole thing. Anything that could shed some light on why someone might want to threaten Destiny.

I was scanning the ground as I thought about all of this, when I noticed a scrap of paper tumbling in the wind. It was probably nothing, but I chased after it anyway. Emergency vehicles were pulling up around me, and I grabbed it right as the first of the firemen leaped out.

"Hey!" he yelled. "What's going on here? Did you call 911?"

I had just enough time to see that it was a hand-drawn map of Firth Academy before I shoved it in my pocket and turned to face the fireman.

"So this some kind of prank?" he said. "Some kind of . . . frat thing?"

His uniform said Officer Emmett, and Officer

Emmett did not seem to be amused. He was a big guy—probably 6'3"—and staring up at his face it was easy to remember the awe with which I'd viewed firemen as a kid. He could probably have bench-pressed me. And right now it looked like he wanted to.

"No sir," I said. "When I called, I really did think there was a person tied to the post. I was far away, and—well, before it burned, it looked a lot more like a person than this."

He looked down at me and sighed. "What were you doing here, anyway?"

"I was just hoping to get a chance to talk to someone on the soccer team about getting involved. There's a big game coming up, and I'm a new student so . . ." I trailed off, trying my best to look like a shy but generally good kid. Thankfully it was a disguise I wore a lot, and I was pretty good at it.

"Kids!" Officer Emmett muttered.

By this point, quite a crowd had shown up. Fire trucks and ambulances were a rare sight on the Firth campus—although they'd unfortunately become more common recently. Students had gathered within minutes, and were busy popping cell phone pictures of the still smoking figure. By afternoon, I had no doubt they'd be all over Facebook. I saw Zeke, my roommate at Firth Academy, in the crowd. He was talking with a long-haired blond student who looked to be about sixteen going on twenty-five. He had some pretty serious stubble. He was one of those tall, classically good-looking guys whose mouth seemed to be twisted in a permanent sneer.

"Yeah," said the blond guy. "Let's see how hot she thinks she is now. She deserves this." He pushed his way to the front of the crowd to snap a few more photos. Then he laughed and gave Zeke a high five.

*Poor Destiny,* I thought. I wondered why that guy had such a grudge against her. I made a mental note to find out more about him. I wondered what Dr. Darity was going to do when he heard about this. This was just what he needed—another big mess on the Firth campus.

As if my thoughts had summoned him, Dr. Darity came walking over. He was moving quickly but stiffly. From the angry expression on his face, it was clear he'd been briefed on what was happening.

Dr. Darity walked right over to Officer Emmett.

"Please take that down," he said through clenched teeth.

"Well," said Officer Emmett, "according to

procedure we should have it checked for finger-prints first."

"I'm fairly certain that no fingerprints could have survived that blaze, Officer. And this is just a prank gotten out of hand. Now, as headmaster of the academy, I would consider it a personal favor if that could be removed. Now."

Dr. Darity was using that overly polite tone that adults sometimes had when what they really wanted to do was scream at each other. It had the intended effect. Officer Emmett yelled at a few of the other firemen, and within a few minutes, they had the figure and the sign down on the ground. This side of the goal was pretty destroyed. They'd have to replace it before any more games could be played here.

Dr. Darity turned to the assembled students and staff. He took a deep breath and ran a hand through his disheveled hair. The crowd quieted, eager to hear what he had to say. He opened his mouth, but someone beat him to it.

"Well!" said a quiet voice from the crowd.

Dr. Darity closed his mouth, surprised. The students parted, and a familiar figure slowly made his way to the front of the crowd. Clad in his usual three-piece tweed suit, leaning heavily on his cane, Dr. Montgomery looked exactly like you'd expect the headmaster of a private school to look. Which made sense, because he'd been head honcho at Firth until just recently.

When he reached the burned remains, he raised a handkerchief to his nose and sniffed loudly, as though he smelled something distasteful.

"Well," he said again. "Well, well, well. All I can say is this is certainly another first in Firth history." He said it with a smile on his lips, but it never reached his eyes.

Dr. Darity didn't seem to know what to say. They were standing shoulder-to-shoulder now. Dr. Montgomery turned to face the crowd.

"Given the events of the past few days, I'm sure Dr. Darity would agree with me that it is a good time to continue the discussion about admissions that was begun earlier this semester."

Dr. Darity tried to interrupt him. "I don't—"

"Have time to hold such a discussion? I understand. The role of headmaster is a demanding one, for certain. Which is why I would be glad to host this discussion at my house, next week. We must all do our part to make sure that Firth continues its legacy as a first-class institution."

*What is he* talking *about?* I thought. I looked at Dr. Darity's face. If he'd been upset before, now he looked like he could kill someone. This was not a topic that made him happy. Whatever this meeting was, it might be a good idea to check it out.

Dr. Darity opened his mouth to say something, but Dr. Montgomery beat him to it again. "What are you all doing standing around here, anyway? Doesn't this school still believe in homework?" He laughed, a cold, dry laugh like wind blowing through a pile of leaves. Then he clapped his hands together loudly. "Dismissed," he said.

Everyone began to wander away in groups of two and three. Dr. Montgomery's housekeeper, Mrs. Wilson, walked over to give him her arm. The two of them headed off without a look back. It seemed like I was the only one to see Dr. Darity, standing forgotten by the remains of the goal, his hands clenched in angry fists.

# 5

## Stakeout

*This mission is really keeping me in shape!* I thought, as Killer and I ran back up the hill I'd just run down, holding the fire extinguisher like a giant baby in my arms. A giant baby made out of lead. Between walking Killer three times a day, and all the other running we'd been doing, I was going to be ready for a marathon by the time this was all over. Although today Killer's three walks had turned into one all-day long walk.

Thankfully, I kept myself in pretty good shape anyway. Which was probably why Destiny had such a crush on me. The girls all go for the MoJoe. Who could blame her, really?

Although it looked like someone blamed her for

something. You'd have to be pretty angry to go to all the trouble of stealing her clothes and making such a crazy mannequin. Was it just because she was a girl at an all-boys' school? Or was it something more? Maybe someone wanted to sabotage the soccer team before the upcoming big game? Or was someone trying to get back at Dr. Darity? There were just too many possibilities and not enough information.

When we finally made it back up to the athletic building, Killer barked at me twice, his ears laid back flat against his head.

"Easy boy," I said, tying him to the tree by the gate. He whined as I slipped past him to return the fire extinguisher. I washed my hands and face quickly in the boys' bathroom to get rid of any lingering smell.

When I returned, I could see the crowds of people beginning to gather by the emergency vehicles on the soccer field. The plume of smoke had died down to just a trickle leaking up into the sky. I untied Killer. We headed in the opposite direction, and he seemed more than happy to get away from the fire.

A thought occurred to me. It looked like everyone was rushing to see what was going on down at the soccer field. Maybe now would be a good time to head back and check out that hut in the woods. If everyone was distracted, no one would notice me sneaking out there. And we needed more information about that place. It was the only link we had with whoever had gone all crazy on the boys' locker room.

Besides, I had to make sure Killer got a good walk, right?

It took about fifteen minutes to get out there, going at a good jog. I took the long way around, through the woods at the edges of Firth Academy, just to make sure no one saw me. Not too long ago Frank and I had run into Charles Westerley, a teacher at Firth, and Killer's old handler, respectively. It didn't take a detective to figure out that their presence at the same place at the same time wasn't a coincidence— they'd been romantically involved and were meeting in the woods in secret. But aside from them, no one seemed to use the paths in the woods much.

Well, them and whoever decided to redecorate the boys' locker room in serial killer chic.

I got lost once or twice on the way—it had been dark last time I was out here, and pretty chaotic— but finally I found the path that I was certain led to that small cabin in the woods. It was all still fresh in my mind: the fight between Ellery and his father, the buckets of blood, the sound of vomiting. Even though it was still daylight out, the woods were dark and still. It made it all the creepier. The only sounds were my quiet footsteps and Killer's heavy, wet breathing.

Finally I caught a glimpse of something up ahead other than trees, trees, and more trees. There was the small clearing I remembered, the broken-down raw wood walls, the one window (painted black, of course). And something I'd forgotten: Mr. Marks's bodyguard.

He was standing there in exactly the same suit (and position!) he'd been in when we left last night. It looked like he hadn't moved a muscle. And boy did he have a lot of muscles. It was like they'd planted an oak tree in front of the door.

I pulled Killer back into the trees a little farther, before the guard could spot us. Mr. Marks had known that we were ATAC agents. It was possible that if I identified myself to the guard, he'd let me into the cabin.

But then again—I still wasn't sure that I trusted Mr. Marks. After all, his son Ellery had turned out to be a psychopath, and he'd tried to help cover it up. And he was a member of this Brothers of Erebus group, whoever they were. While it could just be a harmless part of the fraternity, in my experience, secret societies tend to be full of . . . less than upstanding citizens.

And though I didn't know whether the bodyguard

would let me in, I was certain that whatever he did, he would report right back to Mr. Marks.

I was still figuring out what to do when I heard the sound of someone approaching through the woods.

"Sit," I whispered to Killer. Killer's police training must have included how to behave on a stakeout, because he was as silent as a statue. We both tried to hide as well as we could behind one of the big elm trees. Killer was so still he could have been a rock in the shape of a German shepherd.

Whoever was approaching had reached the edge of the clearing now. I peeked out from behind the tree and saw Spencer Thane—the president of Gamma Theta Theta! Before this I thought he seemed like a pretty decent guy. He'd been out here with us last night when we'd found Ellery. In fact, GTT and Spencer seemed to be at the middle of everything that had been going on recently. And hadn't Destiny said that it was GTT pledges who'd been stealing her clothes? *Interesting . . .*

As I watched, Spencer walked right up to the door of the cabin. The guard gave him the smallest of nods and stepped aside. Spencer walked into the cabin quickly and pulled the door shut behind him. The guard resumed his place in front of the door. Within five seconds it was over, and the little clearing was quiet again.

*If I hadn't been here at just the right moment, I'd have missed everything,* I thought. Seems like I wasn't the only one who realized that the fire provided the perfect distraction if you didn't want to be seen sneaking around in the woods. I wondered what he was up to—and where he was headed after this.

I put my back to the tree and settled into a comfortable position. Killer stayed frozen where he was. Now all I had to do was wait.

And wait.

And wait.

*What is he doing in there?* I thought. It had been nearly an hour since I'd seen Spencer go inside the cabin. It was only one room! There wasn't even electricity, and with that window blacked out, there couldn't have been any light in there. Somehow, I doubted it was his private study room.

Could he be destroying some sort of evidence? I debated rushing the guard, but there was no way I could get past him, and by this point, Spencer would have had the time to destroy whatever he wanted. My only chance to figure this all out was to follow him after he left.

So I waited some more. Now the sun began to

set. The woods, already dark and creepy, became darker and creepier. And then even darker and creepier. And still Spencer stayed in the cabin!

It hadn't been a cold day (for fall), but when you sit in one spot without moving, you get pretty frozen pretty fast. And if it got any darker out, I didn't know if I'd be able to find my way back home, let alone follow Spencer.

Just when I finally decided that he must have moved in to the cabin for good, the door cracked open. In the last bit of daylight, Spencer emerged. I couldn't be sure, but it looked like he was covered in dirt. Had he been rolling around on the ground in there?

Spencer took off at a fast walk through the woods. Killer's ears perked up, and he followed Spencer with his eyes, never moving the rest of his body an inch. *Who's a good dog!* I thought.

*Three Mississippi . . . Two Mississippi . . . One Mississippi,* I counted silently to myself. Finally I quietly started to follow Spencer. He was about thirty feet ahead of me in the woods. This was obviously not the first time that he'd walked through these woods at night. He glided carefully from tree to tree, somehow seeming to avoid the million branches that tore at my face and the rocks that threatened to slip out from underneath me.

Killer was able to keep him in sight. I, however,

was having a harder time. I never would have guessed that I'd be out so late without any light to guide my way, and the trails were still unfamiliar to me. I was lucky to have Killer guiding my way. While he could have no doubt tracked Spencer all across campus, moving quietly through the underbrush was not easy for a two-legged guy without a flashlight. More than once, Spencer paused and looked over his shoulders. Each time, when he started again he walked a little bit faster. Soon he was jogging through the woods.

And that's when I stepped on a dead branch. There were dried leaved and sticks all throughout the underbrush, thanks to the changing of the seasons, but this one was just the right size. Or should I say just the wrong size: small enough for me to break it by stepping on it, big enough to make a sound like a gunshot.

Spencer didn't even bother looking behind him this time. He just took off at a run. Which is when I remembered something else I'd heard about Spencer: Everyone at the Willis Firth Academy was required to take at least one sport. Spencer's was track. And he wasn't just any runner. He was a state champion sprinter who did marathons in his spare time.

He was suddenly moving so fast I thought he was flying. Killer and I took off after him. At first, it seemed like the woods were going to slow

Spencer down. We kept pace with him, falling a tiny bit behind but not that much. I leaped over tree stumps, dodged low-hanging branches, and nearly broke my ankle on a forgotten bit of stone wall. All the while, I managed to keep Killer's leash from getting tangled up on anything.

But every second, Spencer seemed to go a bit faster. He must have been getting used to running in the forest. Soon he was forty feet ahead of us, then fifty, then I could just barely make him out in the distance. If we could just keep him in sight until we were out of the woods, Killer would be able to track him to wherever he was going.

*SMACK!*

I ran straight into a tree. Luckily, my shoulder took most of the impact, but I could tell I'd be black-and-blue tomorrow. Immediately, I tried to locate the slippery shadow of Spencer in the distance, but he was gone.

I turned back to Killer, who was sitting on his haunches with a look that said *nice going*.

"I know," I said. "You don't have to rub it in."

Killer leaned down and ducked his head.

There was nothing I could do about Spencer now; he was already long gone. I turned back in what I hoped was the direction of Killer's kennel. It was going to be a long walk home.

# Under the Radar

Multidimensional Kinetics

A baseball (m = 0.15 kg) is thrown with a
speed of 30 meters per second at angle of
32 degrees above the horizontal. Neglect
air resistance.

a. What is its momentum at the maximum
height?

b. What is its momentum just before it
strikes the ground?

read the problem for a third time. This time I
almost made it to the end before Zeke broke in
on me again.

"I mean . . . just, like wow, right? That thing on

the soccer field. That was wicked sick."

I nodded. Not that Zeke actually seemed to care if I responded. He'd been going on like this all night.

"The way the wig got all melty. That was just gross. I mean grody." He laughed. He didn't seem all that upset about it actually. But then, Zeke didn't seem to get upset about much, except when they'd canceled the dorm-wide pizza party the other night. Pizza was serious business. The murder and harassment of his classmates? That was a laughing matter.

I looked back at my homework. Combined with the craziness of the last few days, my classes appeared to be much more challenging than I'd been prepared for. Firth was no joke and this was seriously not good. Not only would my cover be blown if I didn't keep up appearances of a Firth-worthy scholar, but I'd be seriously behind in my actual classes when I got home.

Finally, it seemed like Zeke had gotten the hint. I actually completed two problems. Zeke was silent for a continuous fifteen minutes—I think it might have been a record.

That's when the music started. Blaring, wailing guitars. It was so loud, I couldn't even tell what it was. Some kind of classic rock I was sure. That was all Zeke ever seemed to listen to. I turned around to find him lying on his bed with his eyes closed. Could he really sleep through all that?

"Zeke? ZEKE? ZEKE!" I shouted his name until he opened his eyes and sat up.

"Sorry man! Couldn't hear you!" He smiled apologetically and pointed toward his stereo. But he didn't make any move to turn it off.

"Can you turn that down? I'm trying to study."

"Oh! Right. Sure." He reached over and turned the knob the tiniest bit. I was no longer bleeding from the ears, but it was still far from ideal. I was about to say something, but Zeke had already collapsed back down on his bed.

I shut my books.

"I'm going for a walk!" I yelled. I couldn't tell if Zeke was nodding because he heard me, or just bouncing his head along to the music.

As soon as I shut the door to our room behind us, I felt better. Like I could hear myself think again. There wasn't really anywhere to go for a walk. After nine o'clock at night, no student was allowed outside of the dorms without express permission of the dean. But now could be a good time to check up on some of the other students.

Joe had filled me in on what he'd seen go down out in the woods, so I decided to start with Spencer.

As a senior and president of GTT, Spencer lived in his very own single in the frat house. I was beginning to understand just how much of a privilege that was. His room was on the top floor of the building in one of the corners. I knocked on the door. He'd already taken physics, so I figured I could use asking him for help as an excuse.

Except he didn't answer. I knocked again. Nothing. There was no light coming from beneath the door, and when I put my ear to the wood, I couldn't hear anything. Maybe he'd gone to bed early? *He did get quite the workout this afternoon,* I thought.

I'd have to check in on him some other time. Luckily, there were a few other people on my list of students to talk to. Lee was up next. Although Destiny was the main target, whoever was pulling these tricks seemed to have some anger left over for Lee, too. Maybe Lee had some enemies he hadn't mentioned before. Being the star of the soccer team, a straight-A student, and GTT's most sought after new pledge, people had to be jealous of him.

I headed over to Lee's dorm. I could tell from down the hall that his door was half open and the lights were on. There was quiet music drifting out into the hallway. I knocked on the door.

"Come in!" yelled an unfamiliar voice.

A guy with long, straight black hair was sitting with his legs up on his desk, reading a book. Had I gotten the wrong room?

"Hi," I said. "Is Lee here?"

"Oh, no man. He's uh . . . at some study group," he said. He turned back to his book, as though he wasn't eager to talk about it.

"Do you know when he'll be back?"

"Nope. Sorry." This time, he didn't even bother to look up from his book. But I could see a blush spread across his face. The guy was definitely lying. But why?

I stood there for a few seconds, hoping that he would say something else, but he was focusing so intently on the book I could have sworn there was steam coming out of his ears. This wasn't going anywhere. I stepped back out into the hallway.

I noticed there were a number of doors that were shut, or rooms with only one person in them. There was definitely a pattern: The guys of GTT—and some of their pledges—were all missing. Looks like they were up to something.

I was on my way back to my room when I noticed something unexpected. Patton was back in the dorm. What's more, he was alone in his room. He was a GTT pledge as well, but clearly not one of the most popular ones. He had to know what was going on. And if he'd been left out, maybe he'd spill the beans. Plus, he was still on our list of suspects.

"Hey Patton."

Patton looked up with a hopeful expression on his face. Then he saw it was just me. "Oh. Hey."

"How's it going?"

Patton shrugged his shoulders and went pack to doodling on a sheet of paper in front of him.

"Are you feeling better?" His face still looked pretty red, but it wasn't the mass of blisters it had been when I'd last seen him.

"I guess. I was in the hospital all weekend, which sucked." In the hospital all weekend, eh? If that turned out to be true, it seemed like Patton was off the hook for the fire at least.

"So . . . where is everybody tonight? This place seems empty."

Patton jerked his head up as if he'd been slapped.

"They're all out doing some stupid GTT initiation thing. I mean, I get my face destroyed for them, and they still pick Lee over me. Just because they're so desperate to have him and they're afraid he'll quit. It's ridiculous!"

"Yeah," I said, trying to hide my excitement. Previous GTT initiation pranks had included stealing the toilet seat from Dr. Darity's office. Maybe they were behind the pranks on Destiny? And Patton was definitely jealous of Lee, and could easily have destroyed the locker room before he ended up in the infirmary. "So what is this initiation thing?"

Patton looked at me suspiciously. He narrowed his eyes. Perhaps he'd realized he'd said too much already.

"It's . . . nothing. Just nothing." He stood up from his chair. "I'm going to bed," he said, and then stretched his arms and gave the fakest yawn I'd ever seen. "Nice talking to you."

Patton nearly pushed me out of his room. Looks like I wasn't getting any more information here. But now that I knew that the members of GTT were out for the night, I had a good idea where I could get some.

Quickly, I made my way back to Spencer's room at the GTT house. After a quick look around to make sure the hallway was empty, I pulled out my bump key—a state of the art spy toy that ATAC had provided to both Joe and I. With old fashioned lock picks, you had to navigate each tumbler in the lock separately, which meant sitting in front of the lock for a long time, with the equivalent of a big neon sign saying BREAKING AND ENTER-ING over your head. With a bump key, you simply slipped it into the lock and tapped it a bunch, until all the tumblers aligned at the same time. Within seconds, easy locks popped right open.

Which is how I found myself in Spencer's room. I slipped the door closed behind me. Thankfully, it was a bright, clear night out. By the light of the moon, I navigated my way across his room to his desk and flipped on the small light.

Spencer's room was so neat it made mine look sloppy. His bed had hospital corners. His books were organized by color and height. Nothing was out of place. I was going to have to be very careful—he was the kind of guy who would notice if anything was out of place.

I whipped out my phone and took a photo of his desk so I'd have something to compare it to when I was done searching and needed to put everything back in its place. Then I started with the drawers. Nothing unusual in any of them—pens, pencils, papers, paper clips. Even his school supplies were laid out in perfect rows. It was so organized it was creepy. I found a gym lock, with the combination written out on a label on its back. Carefully, I put everything back in its place.

His laptop was also on his desk. It powered up as soon as I touched the track pad. Unfortunately, it opened to a password screen. I didn't know much about Spencer, so my chances of figuring out his password were pretty slim. I tried a few things—Spencer, Firth, track. Nothing worked. Then an idea came to me.

I put the laptop to sleep, flipped it over, and searched. No sign of a label. I looked along the back of the screen. Nothing. Finally I pulled out the battery. Bingo! Beneath the battery pack was a small, carefully written label—EREBUS.

There was that word again! Who were the Brothers of Erebus? And what were they up to? They were definitely connected to Gamma Theta Theta, but aside from that, no one seemed willing—or able—to tell me anything about them.

I was about to type in the password when I heard noises in the hallway. Footsteps were approaching Spencer's door. Quickly, I flipped off the light and powered down the computer. In the dark, I waited.

*I'm sure it's just someone going to the bathroom,* I thought. What were the chances that Spencer would come home right now?

Then I heard a hand on the doorknob.

Just my luck. There was no other way out of the room. Right as I heard the lock click, I dove beneath Spencer's bed.

A pair of feet clad only in socks walked across

the floor. Judging from the dirt clinging to the hem of his pants, I'd guess that Spencer took off his shoes outside his room to keep from tracking mud in. He flipped on the same desk light I had turned off just a few seconds earlier, and I held my breath hoping that I'd repositioned everything correctly.

Spencer must not have noticed anything, because he came over and sat down on the bed. The old metal springs creaked and dipped dangerously low, until they were barely half an inch from the tip of my nose. I held my breath, praying it wouldn't dip any lower.

Spencer dropped his backpack on the floor right in front of me. Carefully, I turned my head to look at it. A long piece of wood was sticking out of the end of bag. It was about the thickness of a baseball bat, but rough. One end looked charred, as though it had been set on fire. It was a torch! Destiny had said the brothers of GTT had been playing pranks on her—perhaps today they'd decided to up the ante?

Spencer leaned down to pull some books out of the bag, and I scooted as far back against the wall as I could. He lay down on top of me. I could hear him slowly flipping the pages of his textbook above me.

The floor was cold and dusty and hard. It was going to be a very long night. . . .

---

SUSPECT PROFILE

Suspect: Spencer Thane

Hometown: Atlanta, Georgia

Physical Description: 5'11", 160 pounds, dark skin, super preppy

Occupation: Senior at Firth; head of GTT

Suspected Of: Harassing Destiny Darity, setting fire to a dummy version of her, and running a secret society within GTT known only as the Brother of Erebus.

Possible Motives: Revenge on Dr. Darity for trying to close the frats; revenge on Destiny for being stuck-up and full of drama; or just an old-school desire to keep girls out of Firth Academy.

# 7

## Devoured by Bears

"Don't you ever get bored with this?" I looked down at Killer, who sat at attention, waiting for me to put on his leash. I sighed and clipped him in.

"I mean, it's the same walk every day. Same trees, same buildings. Is it really that fascinating?"

He scratched at the door of the house, eager to get outside.

"Fine," I said. "Don't take my word for it. But I swear, that bush that you love? It's still there. Still a bush."

Killer surged out the door, pulling me after him. Frank was outside waiting.

"So did you find anything out last night?" He

was supposed to call me if he got any information, but I hadn't heard anything from him since I told him about our chase with Spencer.

"Long story," he said. "But yes." He told me about *his* nocturnal adventures with Spencer, and I laughed.

"The whole night? Under his bed?"

Frank rolled his eyes. "Give me a little credit. I managed to slip out once he finally fell asleep. But he sure did study for a while before getting there. Man, my neck hurts."

"Well, he's probably in class now. Should we try his room again?"

"Maybe," Frank replied. "But I checked his computer before I left, and there didn't seem to be anything on it. His password was interesting though. Erebus."

"That name certainly has popped up in a lot of places lately," I said, pulling out my phone.

"I already called ATAC," Frank said, halting me. "They're looking into the Brothers of Erebus. They'll get back with any information they find, as soon as they find it."

"Good call," I said. "In the meantime, I say we go check out the cabin first, see what we can find out about that. Besides, Killer likes the woods. Don't you boy?"

to watch the mannequin of Destiny burn.

"They rehearse in the music building, if that helps. Every night, five o'clock. It's when I take my daily dose of aspirin." Dr. Darity grimaced.

"Good idea," said Frank. "I'm going to tackle the Firth archives in the library—there has to be some kind of clue about a secret society on campus somewhere."

Frank was actually *volunteering* to do library time while I got to hang with the band. He really did love the boring stuff.

"Works for me," I said.

"Thank you boys," said Dr. Darity. "I don't know what I'd do without you."

Frank and I left his office. Frank headed off to class. I headed off to take a nap. This mission was pretty sweet.

A few hours later, refreshed and bolstered by some coffee, I headed out to Alexandra Hall, the Firth Academy music building. It felt nice to be walking around without Killer—for once I didn't have to stop at every interesting tree or bush. It made walking a lot faster.

Lee and Millhouse were already there when I showed up.

"Call me Mill," Millhouse said with a smirk. I could tell right away that I didn't like him, but I

Frank got down on his knees and Killer leaped up on him, licking his face. Killer loved Frank. He acted like a puppy whenever Frank was around.

When we got to the cabin in the woods, Mr. Marks's bodyguard was still there. Did the man ever sleep? Did he have a twin? It was creepy.

We'd decided to just walk right up and see what he did. Maybe Mr. Marks had left special instructions to let certain people in—though that still didn't explain why he'd let Spencer in.

I walked as close as I could to the door, thinking that eventually he would have to say something or move out of my way. Finally, when my nose was about an inch from the guy's chest, I stopped. He hadn't even acknowledged our presence. Behind his mirrored sunglasses, I couldn't even tell if his eyes were open.

After a minute I opened my mouth to say something. The guard spoke first. "Off-limits. Beat it."

"But we—" That was as far as I got.

"Don't care. Leave."

Frank pulled me back from the guy. "Let's talk to Dr. Darity, see if he can get this guy to back off."

"Fine," I muttered, trying not to sound pouty. What good was being a special agent if a glorified traffic cop could push us around?

We headed across campus to Dr. Darity's office.

"Hi boys," he said. "Please tell me you're not here about some new disaster?"

"No," I smiled. "Just the same old disasters."

"We were trying to check out that hut in the woods, but Mr. Marks's bodyguard wouldn't let us in," Frank explained.

"Huh. That's not right. I expressly told him to keep out everyone *but* the two of you. I tried to send him back to Mr. Marks and install school security—but Mr. Marks insisted, and the board of trustees backed him. I'll keep pushing."

"Were you able to find out why the hut is there?" asked Frank, clearly frustrated.

"Or maybe something about the Brothers of Erebus?" I chimed in. "I'm beginning to wonder if there's a connection between the two, but I don't know what it is."

Dr. Darity sighed. "No. That hut doesn't even appear on the maps of the school grounds. And don't even ask about the Brothers of Erebus or whatever they're called. Everyone clammed up when I asked them, and according to all the records I have, they don't exist."

"Don't worry Dr. Darity, we'll figure it out." Frank assured him.

"Do you think there's any chance you can figure it out before the Annual Blair-Firth Soccer[ Cham]pionship and Benevolence Weekend?"

"The what?" That was a lot of words th[at] came out of Dr. Darity's mouth, and I had n[o] what he was talking about. Then I remember[ed] it was that thing everyone was talking about [that] was happening this weekend.

"The big game," Frank translated for me. "[The] Hallie Blair School is the Firth Academy's b[ig] rival."

"That's right," said Dr. Darity. "And the entir[e] Blair school will be coming here on Friday. There'll be a formal dinner, a concert by some student band, and, of course, the big game itself on Saturday."

"It's Lee's band that's performing, right? Devoured by Bears?"

"Yes," said Dr. Darity. "That's them."

"Maybe I'll offer to do their sounding board," I suggested. "I've got some experience and they might need some help with a big event like this. I overheard them talking about a rehearsal this afternoon. Maybe I'll drop by."

It didn't hurt that Lee played drums, and I wanted to keep an eye on him. And the lead singer was a senior by the name of Millhouse Templeton— a.k.a. the obnoxious blond who had been so excited

offered my help anyway, being sure to add that I knew my way around a sound system.

Millhouse's expression made it clear that he'd be surprised if I knew how to operate a cell phone, let alone a sound system. "Are you sure? It might be a little more . . . *sophisticated* than what you're used to."

"Don't mind him," said Lee. "He's just nervous around anyone who wasn't born with a silver iPod in their mouth."

Millhouse laughed.

"Very funny, scholarship boy."

It was a genuine laugh. He might have been an elitist jerk, but at least he was conscious of it.

Just then, the other three members of the band walked in—Albert, Aloysius, and Alastair Alpert. Albert and Aloysius were juniors (and twins), and Alastair was their older brother. Apparently, they'd started the band as a trio, but had opened it up when Lee came to the school, after finding out that he had almost as big a vinyl collection as they did. Albert played keyboard, Aloysius was on bass, and Alastair was guitar. Mill did the vocals and Lee played drums.

After a few minutes of set up, in which I impressed Mill by fixing one of the microphones he'd broken during a recent performance, the band got down to business. After a few warm-up scales, they got going with "Apocalypse the Unicorn," which Lee had told me was their "signature track." They sounded pretty tight.

Or at least, they did for the first two minutes. Then the door to the practice space flew open and Destiny stormed in, a cup of something in her hand. Behind her came a student I'd seen around but didn't know—brown hair, medium build, nondescript.

I could tell from the look on her face and the way her mouth was moving that Destiny was screaming, but it wasn't until the music cut off that I could make out the words.

". . . think it's very funny don't you? I hate you!"

She threw the cup at Mill, and steaming brown liquid ran all down his shirt and pants. Mill started screaming back at her, and I could barely make out a word they were saying. Destiny's friend looked embarrassed. The rest of the band just looked bored.

"I wonder what it's about this time," Aloysius said to Albert. Or was it Alastair? They were hard to tell apart.

"Do they do this a lot?" I asked one of the three. He rolled his eyes and nodded his head.

"This! This is what I'm talking about." Destiny pulled out a bunch of papers from her bag. Someone had written all over them in marker—crude drawings of Destiny on fire, with the words "Drop out of the game and drop out of the skool!!!!"

"I don't know what you're talking about!" Mill responded. "You're so crazy, you probably did that yourself. Just like last time."

*Just like last time?* I wonder what he meant by that.

"Right. I'm crazy, that's what it is. You couldn't possibly just be angry that I dumped you!"

"You dumped me? That's a joke. Everyone in school knows that I kicked you to the curb."

Destiny shoved the papers back in her bag.

"Come on, Casey!" she said. She turned to leave, the other student following close behind her. Right as she got to the door, Mill hurled his microphone at her head. She ducked and it exploded against the wall. It seems Millhouse had quite the temper, and a grudge against Destiny.

After a few seconds of silence, Mill kicked a speaker and took off at a run. Alastair, Aloysius, and Albert all packed up their things and headed out quickly. Soon it was just Lee and me left in the space.

"So . . ." I said. "I guess practice is over?"

Lee laughed. "Seems that way."

"What was all that about?"

"Oh—Destiny and Mill dated earlier in the year, and they've been at each other's throats ever since."

"Do they always fight like that?"

"That was actually pretty easy going, for them. After they broke up, Mill slashed Destiny's tires, and Destiny broke into his dorm room and trashed all of his music."

"And they weren't arrested?"

"Destiny's dad is the headmaster and Millhouse is loaded. The two of them could get away with anything."

Lee started breaking down his drum kit and getting ready to leave. But there was one more thing I wanted to ask him about.

"Who was that other kid? Is he Destiny's new boyfriend?"

"Casey? No, he's another new student. I guess he and Destiny were friends at the Blair School or something."

"It must be hard for him to be here—isn't Blair, like, Firth's big rival?"

"Yeah. I don't know. He seemed pretty standoffish at the beginning of the year, but then he and

Destiny became friends, and he's been rooting for the Firth soccer team ever since. Which is good, because we're totally going to destroy them in the game this weekend."

Lee smiled and packed up the last of his stuff. Soon I was alone in the room, with a lot to think about. Could Mill be Destiny's stalker? He was certainly violent. And he had a good reason to go after Destiny.

---

### SUSPECT PROFILE

Suspect: Millhouse "Mill" Templeton

Hometown: Cape Cod, Maine

Physical Description: 6'1", 180 pounds, blond hair, blue eyes, could be male model

Occupation: Senior at Firth; lead singer of Devoured by Bears

Suspected Of: Trying to threaten, harass, hurt, and possibly kill Destiny Darity

Possible Motives: Destiny and Mill had a bad breakup a few months back—maybe he'd decided that the best way to get over her was to get rid of her?

FRANK

# 8

## No Screaming in the Library

"Wow." The Firth Library was like something out of a movie. It was ridiculous. It was an old stone building at the center of campus, four stories high, with a bell tower at the top. The main door was built like a castle gate: thick wooden planks wrapped in iron bars to keep them together. It was more than a little intimidating.

Inside, it was all dark wood and marble, with high arched ceilings and giant windows. The students sat at long rectangular tables with little lamps on them, or at smaller circular tables hidden in the nooks and crannies of the stacks. There were more books than I'd ever seen in a private library. You could easily fit two or three of the Bayport High School library in the same space. It was like paradise. Except for the abundance of laptops and MP3 players, you could barely tell you were in the twenty-first century.

It was also utterly silent. I could hear my footsteps, and the sounds of pages turning. It was almost creepy. I saw Patton Gage at one of the long tables, hunched over a calculus text book. His face was looking better every day. He waved hello, then went back to working.

I wasn't sure where to get started. I could easily lose myself in here for days. I had to stay on mission. I decided the best bet was to go talk to one of the librarians. Hopefully they'd know where to find everything I needed. I wondered how they found their way around—did they have maps? That's how huge this place was.

At the center of the library I found the reference desk, where an old man sat flipping through a card catalog. I was shocked to see that they still *had* a card catalog—they hadn't gone digital. No wonder Dr. Darity had a hard time finding any information about the Brothers of Erebus. The man looked to be as old as the library itself, with a wrinkled up face, white hair, and a thick pair of horn-rimmed glasses.

"Hi!" I said.

The man looked up, obviously startled. He glared at me.

"Shhh!" he responded. Then he went back to flipping through the cards. I waited for a minute, but it quickly became clear that he considered our conversation over.

"I was wondering if you could help me," I said in my best "good student" voice.

He peered at me through a thick set of glasses, and made a sound deep in his throat. "Hrmph!" Then he pointed to his left. There was a small sign on top of the counter. It read PLEASE SUBMIT ALL RESEARCH REQUESTS IN WRITING. THEY WILL BE ANSWERED IN THE ORDER THEY ARE RECEIVED. YOU ARE NUMBER: 7. The number was written on a small tear-away card, and beneath it were a few lines on which to write requests. There was a mason jar filled with golf pencils next to the sign.

I tore off the slip with the number 7 on it and began to fill in my request. I needed to check out as many histories of Firth Academy as they had— the older, the better. On a whim, I asked to see any old campus maps they might have as well. Maybe I could find out something interesting about that hut while I was at it.

Once I was done, I added my request to a pile of other slips. I watched as the old man pulled a number of cards from catalog. After a few minutes, a young student came to the desk bearing a tall pile of books. He put them down quietly on the counter. The old man stared at them for a second, then dinged a small bell. Another student came and took them away.

The old man gave the first student the cards he had pulled from the catalog, and off he went to fetch them. He must have been a student worker or volunteer. *What a great job,* I thought. Not as great as being in ATAC, but still cool. Then the old man pulled the next slip from the pile of requests. I could tell this was going to take a while.

After half an hour of waiting, I finally had a stack of heavy old books, the kind that were bound in leather and covered in dust. I'd bet they hadn't been opened in decades. I made my way to the back of the library, on the first floor, to one of the more secluded areas. Although it was already quiet, I didn't need any curious eyes wondering what I was researching.

I flipped through a biography entitled *Willis Firth: The Man Who Became Rich on Rabbits*. While it was a thrilling history of fur trapping in the nineteenth century, it didn't quite have what I was looking for. The pictorial collection *The Boys' Schools of New England* yielded little other than an interesting show of uniforms throughout the ages.

Willis Firth's autobiography and a book on the

alumni of Firth Academy's early years also proved similarly useless. I checked the index of each for "Erebus" or "Brotherhood of Erebus," but found nothing. I flipped through the texts, but nothing jumped out at me. This was beginning to seem like a useless exercise.

Then, in a book entitled *An Early History of Firth Academy and Its Natural Environs*, I found a series of survey maps taken of Firth Academy throughout its first one hundred years. In 1932, the campus was expanded to make room for new dormitories, including the Gamma Theta Theta house. In 1934, a small new building appeared on the map. It was labeled GAMMA THETA THETA HUNTING SHED AND TACK ROOM. Five years later, it disappeared from the maps, never to return.

Although I couldn't be certain, I was fairly sure that was the same shed in which we found the blood! It was in the right place—and it was owned by GTT. Which meant it was probably connected to the Brothers of Erebus, somehow. Which would explain why Mr. Marks had put his bodyguard on it, and why the board of trustees was giving Dr. Darity the run around.

I was about to close the book, when I noticed a small note on the last map that had the shed on it. It marked the closing of a series of tunnels that had been planned to connect the various school buildings, allowing students "easy transit during the harsh New England winters." Apparently students had been injured when one of the tunnels collapsed, and in the outcry that followed, all of the tunnels had been boarded up. I felt a tingling in my chest. I had a hunch. . . .

Sure enough, when I finally located a list of the buildings connected by the tunnels, the hunting shed was on it! As were the GTT house, the library, the upper-class dorm, the main student center, and a number of the other older buildings. I had a feeling I knew why Spencer had been in that shed for so long. Had he somehow used the underground tunnels to hide the evidence of starting the fire? Or was he doing something else GTT-related?

I suddenly realized that two other students were near me in the stacks. I could hear them quietly whispering to each other, but I hadn't been paying any attention until I heard one of them say something about "the plan." The other said something I couldn't make out, but it ended with "bring the masks—and the torches."

Plan? Masks? Torches? What were they talking about—and who were they? I stood up quietly and crept closer to the stacks.

"Yeah," whispered one. "We'll make sure this

is the most memorable Benevolence Weekend ever."

The other person laughed. "Right. At least for the Brothers of Erebus it will be."

The Brothers of Erebus! I had to find out who these students were. I carefully began to push the books aside in the stacks, hoping I could peek through the cracks and see them. A smaller book must have been balanced on top of the books I was moving, though, because it fell to the ground. The thump sounded like a gunshot in the quiet of the library. The voices cut off suddenly, and I heard foot steps running off toward the very back of the stacks.

I raced around the side, hoping to at least catch a glimpse of the students, but all I saw was the door to the emergency stairs slamming behind them.

Darn! I ran toward the stairs, hoping I could catch up with them before they'd blended in with the rest of the students studying in the library. But as I grabbed the door handle, I heard screaming coming from behind me!

The screams were high-pitched and sharp. It sounded like someone in terrible pain. I hesitated for a moment, and then turned away from the stairs. I had to help whoever was screaming, and those two were probably long gone anyway.

I ran back to the entrance of the library. Destiny and Casey, a student from my history class, were at one of the private tables. Destiny was on her feet, screaming.

"My hands! My hands! They're burning!"

Her hands were red and blistered, and she was waving them in a desperate attempt to cool them off. There was no sign of a fire, so it had to be some sort of chemical burn. Whatever it was, we had to get it off Destiny's hands, and make sure no one else touched it.

"Casey!" I yelled. "Keep everyone away from Destiny's stuff." Casey stopped staring at Destiny and turned to me. He nodded, and moved to stand between their table and the students who had started to come running over. I grabbed Destiny by the shoulders.

"Listen to me!" I said. "You've got something on your hands. We have to get it off."

I looked her in the eye. Tears were streaming down her face. She bit her lip, but she nodded.

Destiny followed me toward the bathroom, where I had her run her hands under cold water until the burning stopped. They still hurt, but they weren't the throbbing, red mess they'd been a few minutes before.

"Did you touch anything strange? Are you allergic to anything?" *Maybe,* I thought, *it's just a coincidence.*

"Those stupid threats! I'm going to kill Mill for this."

"What threats?" So much for it being a coincidence.

Once she'd washed and dried her hands, she brought me back to the table and showed me the pages from her notebook. Seems like death threats weren't the only thing someone had put on them. Luckily, Casey hadn't touched them earlier, and he'd been able to keep people away from the table until we returned, so Destiny was the only one who'd been injured.

Destiny was certain Mill was the person responsible, but neither she nor Casey had seen him near her bag all day. I managed to steal one of the pages for analysis before Casey wrapped them all up in a spare shirt he had. He put them at the bottom of one of the dumpsters outside the building.

I tried to convince Destiny to tell her father what had happened, but she wouldn't go for it. "He won't believe me anyway," she said. "Besides, Mill's been like this ever since I dumped him. I'll get back at him myself." With that, she left the library.

# The Brothers of Erebus

Getting information about the Brothers of Erebus was harder than trying to find out what embarrassing surprise my parents had planned for my birthday this year. If people knew anything, they weren't talking. And if they were willing to talk, they didn't know anything.

I'd nosed around the other staff, but most of them assumed I was talking about some comic book, or a new superhero movie. Mention of a secret society got me slightly more information— they all seemed to agree that there was some "inner core" to Gamma Theta Theta, but no one had any more information than that. Any group that managed to hide itself from even the cleaning staff was pretty good at keeping a secret.

I sent a text message to ATAC headquarters, hoping they'd turned up something from their database by now. They kept tabs on secret societies and criminal groups of all kinds, from the Illuminati to the Mafia. If the Brothers of Erebus were actually something dangerous, I would have thought for sure ATAC would have some intel on them—but it wasn't like them to take so long in getting back if they had any info to share.

We were also still waiting for the results on the poison-laced paper that Frank had taken from the library. We'd put a tiny square of it into JuDGE for analysis.

The big game was just two days away. Tomorrow was the kick off of the Benevolence Day weekend. If Frank overheard them correctly, the Brothers of Erebus were planning something, and we needed to have some idea of what it was if we were to protect Destiny. So far, we were zero for three on the pranks against her.

Someone has it out for Destiny. But who? She definitely hasn't made any friends on campus, other than Casey it seemed. But whoever did this had to be able to get pretty close to her, in order to get into her notebook to drug it. Mill disliked her because of their history. The members of Gamma

Theta Theta have definitely pulled some pranks on her in the past, and the Brothers of Erebus seem linked to GTT . . . somehow.

I was supposed to meet Frank—for once, without Killer—to go to talk to Dr. Montgomery. As the former headmaster (and like, a truly, really old guy), we thought he might have some information about the Brothers of Erebus. Plus, there was still the whole matter of the "meeting" he had called to discuss admissions. It seemed aimed at Destiny, and scholarship students like Lee, and it made Dr. Darity pretty angry, so there was a chance it could be mixed up in all of this too.

Right as I was about to walk out the door, my laptop beeped. It was a message from ATAC! Destiny's notebook was laced with essence of capsicum—the same oil that made hot peppers hot. Not deadly, but definitely not pleasant. Sadly, it was easy to make. Anyone could go to a grocery store and get the raw materials. Worse, ATAC confirmed that they had no information on the Brothers of Erebus. But they did include one thing, an entry from an encyclopedia of mythology.

> EREBUS: From the ancient Greek,
> meaning darkness or shadow. In Greek

mythology, Erebus was the child of Chaos,
and the living embodiment of darkness.
He was associated with the underworld,
Hades, and death.

"Great," I said out loud. Were we dealing with some sort of death cult? Revenge, jealousy, anger, money—I could understand all of these motives. But scary cults just creeped me out. Wait till I told Frank about it. He'd probably want to go learn Ancient Greek as a first step to our investigation.

"You know," said Frank, "it could be pretty helpful if one of us knew some Greek. Just in case. They might conduct their rituals in Greek. Or pass hidden notes in Greek. I wonder if there's a Greek class at Firth?"

I groaned. I knew he'd go there.

We were walking across campus toward the Cottage, which is what they called the retired headmaster's house. All around us were signs of people gearing up for the Benevolence Weekend. Someone had built a giant papier-mâché replica of Killer, and posted it on the main quad chasing a much smaller version of the Blair School mascot, a Bengal tiger. There were banners hanging from all the dorms that read "Go Killers!" and "Defeat Blair!" Seems like they took this rivalry pretty seriously.

Outside the student center, preparations of another kind were in full swing. All the windows were being washed, and a number of fancy tables were being set up for the big dinner. The pathway had been lined with dozens of four-foot-tall torches. They didn't look anything like the one I had seen in Spencer's bag, but they still gave me a chill. Someone out there had their own plans for this weekend, and I had a feeling the preparations were a lot more dangerous.

Finally, we reached the rectory. Mrs. Wilson, Dr. Montgomery's housekeeper, was scrubbing the outside walls of the house. It looked as though someone had spray painted graffiti all over them. Mrs. Wilson had cleaned off the majority of it, though, so I couldn't tell what it had said.

"Hello, Mrs. Wilson," I said. She didn't even turn to look at Frank or me. She just kept right on working. She sniffed audibly as we went by. She was one of the few members on the staff who had never been friendly toward me. She didn't even eat with the rest of us, preferring to eat with Dr. Montgomery or find a table on her own if she had to eat in the cafeteria. I could only imagine how much fun it must have been to have her around twenty-four-seven. Dr. Montgomery was one lucky guy . . . *not!*

I slipped past her and knocked on the front door. It opened a few seconds later.

"Hello boys," said Dr. Montgomery. "Please do come in."

He pointed toward a small living room at the front of the house, and Frank and I walked in. It was dimly lit, and everything had an old, antique— but very clean—feel to it. It was obvious that Mrs. Wilson took her job seriously. Dr. Montgomery limped along slowly behind us.

"What brings you here today?" he asked, settling into a chair and gesturing for us to have a seat.

"I was doing some research on Firth history, for a project," said Frank. "And I was wondering if you could help me out?"

This was the cover story we had come up with— Frank was doing a history project, and I was simply interested in learning more about the school I was working for. It wasn't our best, but we didn't have a lot of time to make it up.

"Really?" said Dr. Montgomery. "How wonderful. I always hope our new students will take more of an interest in the history of the school. What class did you say this was for?"

"History," said Frank.

"Of course. And you would be a junior?"

Frank nodded. He looked worried.

"That's quite interesting. I wouldn't have imagined that Mr. Martinelli would allow a paper on Firth for his juniors, considering that the class is on European history."

"I'm doing it as extra credit." Frank didn't even bat an eye. Every adult in the world looked at Frank and saw a perfect golden child, which made it all the easier for him to be a great liar.

"What happened outside?" I asked, deciding that he might need some help.

"Oh." Dr. Montgomery's face darkened. "Some student vandals, I'm sure. Ruffians."

*Wow,* I thought. *Who says "ruffians" anymore?*

"Not to worry though," continued Dr. Montgomery. "The indefatigable Mrs. Wilson will conquer the forces of mess once again. The meeting will go on."

"Right," said Frank. "That meeting. I heard you announce it the other day. What's it all about?"

"The Willis Firth Academy is a renowned institution, as I am sure you are both aware."

He paused, waiting for some answer. Frank and I quickly nodded.

"During my tenure as headmaster," he continued, "I saw an unprecedented growth in the student population—all good students, from good families."

Another pause.

"That's what we hear," I said.

"You see, the job of headmaster at Firth is a serious task—there is responsibility to uphold, reputation to maintain." He smiled, as though he were thinking of fond memories. "In my fifth decade of headmastership, the board of trustees agreed that it might be best if I stepped ~~down to allow another~~ highly qualified candidate to take over the reverent position."

"Dr. Darity, you mean?"

"Yes, Dr. Darity. Darity never did attend Firth," Montgomery said through his teeth. He brushed invisible crumbs from his lapels. "But I respect the trustees of this school and know that they are doing their best to put Firth first. If Dr. Darity felt as though he were the best candidate for the job, I trusted them."

Frank eyed me suspiciously. We'd both noticed the past tense usage of the word "trust."

"My views and policies have made me enemies before, but we must maintain our standards, boys. Besides, if my enemies are the sort of cowards who would destroy a man's home rather than debate him in public, it merely shows the virtue of my cause. Am I correct or am I not?"

"What kind of views have been disputed to the point of making enemies?" Frank asked, expertly avoiding

Dr. Montgomery's clearly rhetorical question.

"Oh, the age-old debates. Monetary requirements and the like. High standards is all it is."

"So you don't think the school should take scholarship students?" I asked. "But isn't Lee one of the best students at Firth right now? Star soccer player, great grades—"

"Clearly, you boys are too young to understand the issues." Dr. Montgomery had pursed his lips into a hard, straight line. But he paused and smoothed his lips into a tentative smile.

"Anyway," he continued, "I'm forgetting my manners. Your . . . history project, was it?" His tone was once again the welcoming, grandfatherly one he had employed before.

"That's right," Frank said.

Dr. Montgomery laughed. "Let's cut to the chase, shall we boys? I know all about your little club. ATAC, isn't that the name?"

Frank looked like he'd been slapped.

Would Dr. Darity have shared details of our investigation with Dr. Montgomery? What part of "secret agent" didn't these people understand? Either way, our cover was blown. And Dr. Montgomery was clearly not a man who enjoyed being toyed with.

"Yes, sir," I jumped in. "American Teens Against

Crime. We have a need-to-know authorization policy, which is why we had to employ this cover story. It's not personal. There are lives at stake."

Dr. Montgomery nodded thoughtfully.

"We're trying to find out about the Brothers of Erebus." Frank had finally gotten his voice back. "We think they might be involved in some of the incidents that have occurred around campus recently. Can you tell us anything about them?"

Dr. Montgomery laughed. "The Brothers of Erebus? I didn't even know they were still around. They're a harmless club. In fact, in my day, they were a positive influence on the school. A few of the older, wiser students, helping to direct the efforts of the younger. The Brothers of Erebus simply recognizes that certain people are born leaders, and others are born to be followers. I'm sure you understand. ATAC must have some leadership, no doubt."

Dr. Montgomery had a smile on his face, but I still wasn't sure I trusted him about the Brothers of Erebus. They were definitely still around, and as for harmless . . . well, only time would tell.

"Well, it was a pleasure to speak with the two of you. I do, however, need to get ready for tonight. I'm sure you can find your way out."

Dr. Montgomery struggled to his feet. A rush of

cold air swept in, and I turned to see Mrs. Wilson holding the front door open for us. I wondered how long she'd been standing there, and what she'd heard. We might as well get name tags that said "secret agents."

Clearly, it was time for us to leave.

# Field of Screams

After our less-than-successful visit with Dr. Montgomery, both Joe and I decided we needed to blow off some steam. Joe headed back to take Killer on a long walk, while I decided to go check out soccer practice. Watching other people kick things hard was the next best thing to getting to do it myself.

On the way, I thought about what Dr. Montgomery had said. If there really were a lot of people upset by Destiny or scholarship students like Lee being at the school, it was possible we might be after multiple suspects. That made our work all the harder—and meant that the best way we could catch whoever was responsible was to keep an eye on Destiny and Lee.

The team was just warming up when I got over to the athletic field. While they stretched, I decided to check around the grounds and get a good sense of the area. Since both Lee and Destiny spent a lot of time out here, it seemed likely that whoever was out to get them would strike here at some point.

The main athletics building had an indoor gym, a pool, a weight room, all the coaches' offices, and the boys' locker room (which had finally been cleaned and repaired). Everything looked in order—or at least as much as a place used by a hundred guys on a daily basis ever looked to be in order.

The school had made a separate changing room for Destiny, inside one of the caretaker's houses that was currently not in use. Unfortunately, it wasn't very near the soccer field. Instead, it was tucked away by itself behind some trees, about five minutes away. On the walk over, I couldn't help but notice how isolated it seemed, even on the middle of campus. Between the hills and the trees, a game could be going on down at the soccer field, and no one would have any idea what was happening up here. It definitely made me worried for Destiny's safety.

When I got to the house, I tried the door, but it

was locked. Dr. Darity had told us that Destiny had the only key. I just hoped whoever had the chance to lace her notebook with poison hadn't thought to take it and make a copy. As much as I could tell from the outside, everything looked normal. I decided to head back and check out the practice.

Since the game was less than forty-eight hours away, and tomorrow's practice was cancelled because of the Benevolence Weekend opening dinner, the soccer team was hard at work when I returned. And *hard* was definitely the word for it. This wasn't one of the friendly practices I was used to at Bayport High. They had divided up into two teams, and were playing a full on game. They looked like they were out to kill each other, with brutal slide tackles and "accidental" body checks. The way they passed the ball, they were lucky no one had broken an ankle yet. It was intense, and great to watch.

Although everyone was good, one team was destroying the other, thanks to two players who stood out among the rest. Lee seemed to be everywhere for the offense—passing the ball, stealing it from the other side, running rings around the defense, and mostly, scoring. For every point any other play on the team got, Lee seemed to get at least one. He was on fire.

In fact, he was almost as impressive as Destiny. Standing within the rebuilt goal post with her hair pulled back in a pony tail, she looked tiny, but nothing could get past her. She blocked the ball with her hands, her head, and her body. I watched her dive straight into the ground to stop a ball that looked to be going about one hundred miles an hour. She didn't even flinch, just picked it up and tossed it back out to the defense. She was a machine, despite what had happened to her hands just yesterday.

Finally, the coach called a break. While most of the guys walked off together, or sat in small groups drinking water, Destiny stood off on the sidelines by herself. I hurried over to talk to her while I had a chance.

"Hey!"

Destiny jumped when I put my hand on her shoulder. She turned, and relaxed when she saw it was me. For all her brave talk, it seemed like she might be a little more nervous than she let on.

"Hi Frank. How's it going?"

"I'm ok—how are *you*?" I looked at her hands. They still looked a little red, but they mustn't have been hurting her too badly. She put them behind her back when she saw me glance at them. Clearly, it was the wrong question to start with.

She tensed back up before answering me.

"I'm good. It's, whatever, you know?"

"How are your hands?"

"They're fine. Lighten up. Stuff happens. I gotta concentrate on the game. Where's your cute brother?"

It was clear she didn't want to talk about the pranks.

"Are you excited about the game?" I wanted to keep her talking, just on the off chance she might mention something important.

"Yeah! I'm excited to get to destroy those Blair School idiots. Finally a chance to get back at them." She crushed her plastic Dixie cup in her hand as she spoke.

"Didn't you used to go there?"

"Yeah, but they kicked me out for something totally stupid. I'm just glad they sent over my old blood supply from their health center so I could play. They are sooo irritated to be playing against me, too. People have been sending me text messages that say 'tr8or!' all week. Believe me, those stupid threats are nothing compared to what I had to deal with before I left Blair."

Interesting. If she was getting threats from her old school, maybe they had something to do with the pranks, too.

"What about Casey? Didn't he go to Blair too?"

"Yeah, but he says he, like, hated it there, and we're cool now. I was kind of shocked really. We'd never been friends before. But he's a good guy. Unlike some people around here."

"So you're not worried at all?"

"Look, I got to get back to practice. Thanks for saying hi."

With that, she tossed the crumpled cup in the garbage and headed back out to the center of the field. It seemed weird that she wasn't concerned about everything that was going on. But then, with the way she concentrated on the game, maybe she just didn't have time to think about much else.

I looked across the field as the players started to get ready to play again. They'd replaced the goal almost overnight, but you could still see the scorched remains of the grass beneath it. Hopefully no one would notice during the game.

A movement caught my eye, and I looked up at the top of the hill above the soccer field. The truck that painted the white lines on the field was parked up there. It was moving very slowly toward the edge of the hill. It wasn't on the road. And there didn't seem to be anyone behind the wheel!

I looked down at the soccer field. No one had noticed the truck was moving—they were all so intent upon the game. I looked up again. It was definitely moving faster, and it was almost on the hill itself. Their must have been someone behind it, pushing. Once it started heading downhill, it would be unstoppable. And unless my math skills had totally failed me, it was angled to run directly through the goal Destiny was standing inside! It was behind her, and she'd never see it before it crushed her.

I had to get to that truck. It was shooting down the hillside at this point, going faster and faster by the second. I took off at high speed, running toward the hill. I made it to the base and then paused. I only had one chance to get this right. If I didn't time it properly, I was going to end up as road kill—and so would Destiny.

Behind me, I could hear the game going. No one had realized anything was wrong. In front of me, the truck was only fifty feet away. Then forty. Then twenty. When it was ten feet away, I got ready to jump.

Five . . . four . . . three . . . two . . . one!

"OOMPH!"

I leaped in the open window of the truck. My chest slammed against the door. I didn't make it all the way inside, but thankfully, I didn't need to. I yanked the wheel, turning the truck to the right.

And just in time—it shot directly past the goal, narrowly avoiding hitting anyone on the field.

*Now,* I thought, *I just need to hang on and avoiding getting crushed.*

Thankfully, once it was off the hill the truck started to slow down. Someone must have taken off the emergency break and given it a push to get it started. And whoever did it was aiming right for Destiny.

The truck finally rumbled to a halt about fifty feet from the field, and I dropped off. I was going to have a wicked bruise on my chest tomorrow, but aside from that, no one was hurt.

"Are you all right?" Destiny was the first person to reach me. Lee was right behind her.

"Quick thinking man! You okay?" asked Lee.

"I'm fine."

*TWEEEET!* The coach blew his whistle. "Everyone back up! I know CPR. Son, are you all right?"

I explained again that I was fine. The coach took one look at the truck and shook his head.

"Maintenance! I'm always trying to tell them to be careful. Somebody could have gotten hurt by accident. Say—you've got pretty quick reflexes. Want to join the team next year?"

I shook my head. The coach shrugged and blew his whistle again.

"All right! Nothing to see here. Back on the field!"

Somehow, I didn't think this was an accident. I hadn't seen anyone up on the hill, nor had there been anyone suspicious around earlier. But if people were using these hidden tunnels to get around, they could be anywhere, and I would never know.

It was a long walk back to the dorm with that thought in my head. Every few feet, I thought I saw someone moving out of the corner of my eyes. I'd turn around, and it would just be the wind in the trees or a bird. But I knew that somewhere beneath me, people were moving. People up to no good.

## Bringing Down the House

Even though I was worried for Destiny, I was excited when Friday finally rolled around. Tonight would mark the beginning of the Annual Firth-Blair Benevolence Weekend, which meant two things.

First, if what Frank had overheard was true, the Brothers of Erebus were plotting something. This was our big chance to catch them in the act and bust them for good. We'd be saving Destiny, too—which would hopefully mean some more time to hang out with her. I'd barely seen her in the past week, ever since she'd called me cute and said she wanted to date me to make her dad angry. I was hoping she'd be even more interested once I'd saved her life. After that, we could get out of here, which meant no more dog duty (or doodie) for me.

But even better than saving Destiny's life, busting the Brothers of Erebus, and getting away from Killer, tonight meant something else: party! This school was a little stodgy for me—except when it came to killing—and it seemed like they could really use some fun.

"I can't wait for the party tonight," I said to Frank as we got ready in his room. Neither of us had tuxedos, so we'd had to borrow some. Luckily, Firth Academy kept some on hand for just such an occasion. "Finally, a chance to have some fun on this mission."

"Fun?" says Frank. "If by fun you mean an incredibly stressful evening full of new people who may or may not be trying to kill some students on campus, then I totally agree."

"Sure, sure. There could be death. But there will definitely be cake! And music. You haven't heard Devoured by Bears yet—they're really good."

"Well . . . I guess I do like cake."

Frank smiled and gave me a high five. I checked us out in the mirror. We looked good in the tuxedos, I had to say. Very James Bond. Ladies, look out. There were some superspies headed your way.

Oh, that's right. The other exciting thing about tonight? The Hallie Blair School was coed. Which meant that after dinner, during the Devoured by Bears show, there would be dancing. Like, with girls.

Once we were all decked out, we headed off toward the Marks Student Center—named after the great-great-grandfather of Ellery Marks, who had recently managed to accidentally kill and wound a number of his fellow students. I couldn't help but think it was a bad omen.

I reached down and slipped a bow tie onto Killer's collar. He was coming to the party tonight, so he might as well be dressed properly. If anything went down tonight, he'd already shown himself to be good backup. Plus, girls loved dogs. It was a proven fact. Killer was my in.

When we got to the party, it was crazy. Between the Firth Academy students and the newcomers from The Hallie Blair School, there were nearly three hundred people in the room. Thankfully, the great hall of the Marks Building was like the size of an airport. So even with all the tables for dinner, and the stage set up for the band, there was still room for people to wander around and mingle. There were waiters passing trays of fancy finger food and champagne flutes full of sparkling apple cider.

"Okay," I said to Frank. "I could get used to this."

About ten seconds later, I was mobbed by three girls from the Blair School. They surrounded me on all sides, exclaiming at a high pitch.

"He is the cutest!"

"Look at his little face."

"Who's a good guy?"

Sadly, they were talking about Killer, not me. Frank wandered off through the crowd, trying to find Destiny so he could keep an eye on her. Usually, she stood out in the crowd of guys that was Firth Academy, but tonight, she was one woman among many. Maybe Frank was right about this being tricky.

Killer provided the perfect opening, though, so I chatted with a few of the Blair students about Destiny. Maybe they would know if there was anyone in particular we should watch out for.

"Ugh!" said one. "She's such a total loser."

"Yeah," another added. "Mean as a snake, too."

"And she always needs attention. Me, me, me—that's Destiny."

It looked like we might have to protect her from *all* of the Blair students. The three of them seemed ready to go on all night about how much they hated Destiny. Thankfully, Dr. Darity came on over the microphone. "If students could please find their seats, dinner will be served momentarily."

I pulled Killer away from the girls, and headed over to the Firth staff table. They'd hired special caterers for one night only, so that "everyone in the Firth community" could take part in the celebration. We were all the way at the back of the ballroom, as far from the stage as possible. But there was one perk: we were the closest to the kitchens.

This wasn't a normal cafeteria meal, either. The school had gone all out to impress their rivals. Soup, salad, steak, lobster, lamb, roasted vegetables . . . dish after dish was brought to the table. I ate until I thought I would explode. And then they started bringing out desserts: chocolate mousse, strawberry shortcake, ice cream, and apple pie. This was my kind of meal!

As we were eating dessert Dr. Darity took the microphone again.

"I'd like to thank everyone for being here tonight, especially our esteemed colleagues from the Hallie Blair School. This weekend has been a tradition going back more than one hundred years, and we are proud to continue it tonight."

There was a polite smattering of applause, though most people were too busy finishing off their desserts to really put much energy into it.

"And of course, tomorrow will be the big game, which I know you're all excited for."

That was a much bigger applause line. The entire soccer team clapped and stomped in rhythm—they must have practiced ahead of time. It took Dr. Darity a few minutes to get the room to quiet down again.

"Now, I know you're all excited for the concert to begin, but we have one more order of business before we can get to that: the Excellence Awards. Every year, Firth celebrates our best students—academically, physically, socially."

One of the other staff nudged me in the side. "Funny how he doesn't mention the real reason they do this tonight: it's a good chance to thumb their noses at the Hallie Blair School. They're always trying to one up each other and show off their students."

For the next thirty minutes, Dr. Darity read off the names and achievements of students at the Firth Academy. Highest GPA, Best Athlete, Most School Spirit. The list went on and on. Surprisingly, Frank's roommate Zeke won the Student Poetry Award. I didn't think he even knew what poetry was! He looked pretty embarrassed when he accepted it. I had a feeling I wasn't the only one he'd been hiding his artistic side from.

Finally, Dr. Darity got to the main event. The Willis Firth Spirit Award, given to the student who best exemplified the ideals of Firth Academy. Dr. Darity went on and on about how much the award means, how this person must show intelligence, leadership, morals, and everything that is good and pure in the world. He explained that former recipients had gone on to be senators, governors, even a Nobel Prize winner. Finally the big moment came.

"This year's recipient of the Willis Firth Spirit Award is . . . Lee Jenkins!"

There was thunderous applause from around the room as Lee walked up to the platform to receive the award. Aside from whoever had trashed his locker, Lee was almost universally loved at the Firth Academy. And from what I'd seen so far, he deserved the award more than anyone else on campus.

"Gee, thanks," said Lee, blushing. The room cracked up laughing. "No, really," he continued. "I never in my life thought I'd get to go to a school like this, growing up where I did, with no money. So this means a lot to me. And I'd like to thank everyone who helped me fit in here at Firth. And most especially Dr. Darity, who made it possible for me to go here at all."

Lee turned to Dr. Darity and began applauding him. After a second, the entire room joined in. One by one, people began to get to their feet. Soon, Dr. Darity was getting a standing ovation from nearly the entire room. I couldn't help but notice that sourpuss Mrs. Wilson was the only person at the staff table still seated. Did she like anyone other than Dr. Montgomery? I noticed Patton wasn't standing either. He had a jealous frown on his face. Looks like maybe he was hoping to win the Spirit Award himself.

Once Lee got off the stage, people were up and mingling again. All of the winners were mobbed with congratulations, but Lee had the biggest line of students and teachers coming up to him. Even some of his opponents on the Blair soccer team came up to shake his hand! He really was that well liked.

While everyone was standing, the caterers began to clear away all the tables and chairs. Up on the stage, I saw Mill, Albert, Aloysius and Alastair begin setting up the equipment for the concert. I hopped up on stage to give them a hand. I'd be sitting behind the band tonight, running the sound board.

"I wonder if they'll let Lee alone long enough for him to get changed and help set up," said Alastair. Or was it Albert? I still had a hard time telling them apart.

"I'm just hoping they let him go long enough to play! Look at that line." Mill pointed to the audience. You'd have thought that Lee was some celebrity from the way people were competing to shake his hand.

Finally, Lee was free from all the congratulators. He hopped up on the stage and took off his tuxedo jacket. From behind the curtains, he lugged out his drum set piece by piece. Once all of the instruments and the sound board were hooked up, he and I each grabbed an end of the giant DEVOURED BY BEARS sign that the band had made, complete with their logo—a stylized version of the Willis Firth Academy with a bite taken out of it.

Soon all of the equipment was in place. The band started warming up and I took my seat behind the mixing equipment at the back of the stage. From here, I had a great view of the entire audience. Almost all of the tables and chairs had been broken down by now, and the students had removed their jackets and ties. Everyone was in the mood to party. Even the soccer players, who all needed to be at their best for the game tomorrow, looked ready to dance all night.

I could see Frank in the middle of the crowd, toward the right hand side. I looked around him, and sure enough, there was Destiny, five feet ahead.

I felt glad Frank was near her. I could keep an eye on her from here, but if something happened, I'd be too far away to be of any help. I had handed Killer over to Frank since the dog was so in love with him, and he was behaving like a perfect angel by Frank's side. Figured.

The band struck up the opening notes of their first song, and the crowd let out a howl. When these buttoned up prep-school types had a party, they really knew how to get down! Within a minute, the room had become a seething mass of tuxedos and dresses, sweat and hair. The room had amazing acoustics, and the band was on fire. The energy of the audience seemed to energize them, and vice versa. The sound just kept getting stronger and better by the second!

Mill was singing and screaming louder and louder. The vibe of the audience seemed to flow right into him, and he was whirling around along with them. He jumped up and down, ran across the stage, and generally acted like a man on fire—and the crowd loved it!

The big finale of the first song came. Mill leaped straight up in the air on the final note, and came down right at the dead center of the stage. There was a terrible shattering noise. Mill screamed—and went straight through the floor!

## The Secret Passage

After Joe handed Killer off to me, I quickly made my way over to where Destiny was hanging out. Usually she had Casey with her, but tonight he was nowhere to be found. I almost felt bad for her.

"Hey Destiny," I said, walking over.

"Buzz off." She waved her hand at me, like a queen issuing an order.

"Excuse me?"

"Look, I don't need your pity. I don't need friends. I'm actually enjoying just for once not being the only girl on campus, and having a hundred guys staring at me. Plus, I was in here all day helping my dad set everything up and I'm tired. So please, leave me alone."

I walked off, a little offended. But I could understand what she meant. It must have been hard to be the only girl and the subject of so much harassment. Still, she didn't need to be a jerk about it. But I guess that was how she got by.

I managed to stay near her for most of the evening. I couldn't sit with her at dinner—she was up at the headmaster's table with her father, Dr. Montgomery, and the headmaster of the Hallie Blair School—but I took the table nearest to them. As luck would have it, Lee was sitting there as well, so I could kill two birds with one stone.

Patton was sitting at a table nearby, trying his best to get Spencer to talk to him. It was the first time I'd seen Spencer since I'd nearly gotten caught in his room. He avoided meeting my eye, and I made a mental note to try to talk to him when dinner was over. Casey, I noticed, was sitting over with some Blair students. Unlike Destiny, they still seemed to like him.

Everything seemed fine throughout dinner. Killer lay on the floor at my side, drooling when I cut into the steak but well behaved as usual. When Lee was given the Willis Firth Spirit Award, our whole table exploded into applause.

During the standing ovation, Spencer must

have slipped out of the room. When the award ceremony was over and everyone stood up, he was gone. But there was nothing I could do. Joe was already on stage helping set up for the band, and someone had to keep an eye on Destiny. Still, it was definitely suspicious.

I positioned Killer and myself near Destiny in the crowd as the band started. Everything Joe had said was true; they were incredible—for about three minutes. Then came the horrible crashing sound, and Mill disappeared through the stage floor.

For a moment, everyone was still. No one was sure if it was part of the act or not. Then Killer let out a low growl, and Mill started screaming. "Help! My legs! Someone help!"

I tried to fight my way through the mass of people, but it was madness. Some people were rushing toward the stage, others were rushing away. People were screaming. Dr. Darity and the faculty were trying to get the students to calm down. By the time Killer and I finally fought our way to the front of the room, Joe was already climbing down into the hole in the floor. Lee and the other band members were starting to follow him. Luckily, ATAC trained us in the latest paramedic procedures.

"Guys," I called out to the four of them. "I need you to make a circle around the hole, facing outward. Don't let any random students through." The most important thing was to give Joe room and time to assess the situation. Having a thousand people trying to rush over and assist would be the opposite of help.

"Lee, I want you to get on the phone and call the paramedics."

Lee, more than any of them, seemed calm enough to talk to emergency services.

"Joe?" I called down the hole.

"He's alive! But I think he's broken both legs. They're going to need a stretcher to get him out."

Dr. Darity had made his way through the crowd by this point. I grabbed his arm and pointed him toward the microphone. "Mill is going to be all right. Get everyone to calm down and exit the building."

He seemed thankful to have something to do. After a few false starts, he was able to quiet the frightened crowd and convince them to leave the premises. He also assured them that, despite this terrible accident, the big game would continue tomorrow.

Finally the ambulance arrived and carried the now unconscious body of Mill out of the ballroom. Joe was right—he'd broken both his legs, as well as a wrist and his collarbone. Though none of the injuries were life threatening, it would be quite some time before he would walk again.

Once he was safely removed from the premises, I pulled Lee aside. "You guys were in here rehearsing earlier, right?

Lee nodded.

"Did you see anything strange? Was anyone hanging around?"

"No. There was nobody else here but us, and the people who were setting up. Is—is Mill going to be all right?"

"I think he'll be okay," said Joe, who had come up from behind while we were talking. "And you didn't notice anything wrong with the floor then?" Joe asked Lee.

"I mean, I didn't really notice the floor at all. It's just, like—the floor, you know? Look, I've got to get some sleep before the game tomorrow. Is it okay if I take off?"

I nodded. It didn't seem like Lee knew anything that would be useful.

The room had emptied out. Only Dr. Darity, Destiny, Joe, Lee, Killer, and myself remained. Joe pulled Dr. Darity aside to ask him for permission to examine the stage before the police were called—and to tell him to keep an eye on Destiny. Lee offered to walk Destiny home, and Dr. Darity went to his office to call Mill's parents.

Once they were gone, I began to examine the hole itself. It only took a moment to confirm my worst fears.

"Joe, look." I pointed to the edges of the hole. The break in the floorboards was clean on one side, not the jagged edge one would imagine if the wood had simply broken underneath the weight of his jumping. Someone must have sawed through the wood to weaken it. Mill had been set up.

"Why Mill? Who would want to hurt him?" I wondered aloud.

"I don't know," said Joe. "None of the other incidents have been aimed at him. He is kind of mean, but still . . ."

"If he hadn't landed just right, this would have killed him. Whoever did this meant business."

I hopped down into the hole. It was dark here, beneath the stage. Thankfully there was enough light from the hole in the floor to be able to see. The room was filled with swirling dust and splinters—and about a century's worth of leftover props and scenery from various shows that had been put on by the Firth Drama Society.

Silently, Joe and I canvassed the room. In a place

as messy as this, there was only one way to do a proper search: slowly and carefully. We divided the room into a grid, like a spreadsheet, and slowly searched each quadrant.

"Frank!" From the way Joe called my name, I could tell it was important. I abandoned the thing I'd been searching—a seven-foot-tall castle, complete with a working drawbridge—and rushed over, Killer at my heels.

"Look." Joe was holding up a long piece of velvet curtain. Underneath it was a saw. Unlike everything else in the room, it wasn't covered in dust. I looked closer. There was wood caught in some of the teeth. It had been used recently—and I was pretty sure I knew where.

Something bright next to the saw caught my eye. It was a black-and-silver scrunchie, exactly like one I'd seen Destiny wearing at soccer practice in the past! But I couldn't remember the last time I saw her with it. Joe and I stared at it in silence for a second.

"No way," said Joe, when he saw the look on my face. "I don't think Destiny could have done this. Besides, there were a lot of girls on campus for Benevolence Weekend. This could belong to anyone."

"Yeah," I agreed. "But how many of them have a

reason to hate Mill? And have gotten into physical fights with him before?"

Then I noticed something. There was a spot of blood on the scrunchie. Whoever had worn it must have cut themselves sawing. This could be just the clue we needed. I pulled JuDGE out of my pocket. Since they'd already been able to identify Destiny's blood once, we'd get a match if this was hers.

"Always prepared, eh?" Joe smiled.

"Like a boy scout," I agreed. "Only way cooler."

I took a few photos on my cell phone of everything just as we'd found it, for evidence purposes. Then I carefully rubbed JuDGE's sensor on the blood spot.

"If this is Destiny's blood, we'll know soon."

I lifted the scrunchie up with a pen, careful not to get my fingerprints on it. I put it in my pocket. The saw we'd have to come back for—my backpack didn't fit with the formal-wear theme of the evening.

"Do you feel that?" Joe asked suddenly.

"Feel what?" I said. But then I stopped. There was a cold breeze coming from one corner of the room—which didn't make any sense, as the basement had no windows or doors to the outside.

"Frank, was the Marks Student Center on that list you found of places connected by the underground tunnels?"

I thought for a second. "Yeah, it was."

Joe followed the breeze back to the far corner of the room. There was a pile of old huge props leaning against the wall. The breeze got stronger the closer we got to it. At first it looked like they would be impossible to move. But on inspection, they were balanced perfectly on one point. With just a little pressure they moved.

The source of the cold air was revealed to be a small wooden door!

"I think I know how our culprit got in here," Joe said. "And I think I know how we're going to find them."

# Things That Go Bump in the Night

I took the leash from Frank and let Killer lead the way as we headed down into the tunnels. Who knew what we might run into down there. Having a trained police dog with us might come in handy.

"Come on boy," I said. "We need you."

Downstairs, Frank had cleared away all of the debris in front of the doorway.

"In case we need to make a quick exit," he said.

By the time I'd gone five feet into the tunnel, I couldn't see my own hand in front of my face. It was pitch black down there. Thankfully Killer didn't seem to have any problem. Whether he was finding the way by sight or smell, I couldn't tell, but he was at the forefront of our little party from the moment we entered the tunnels.

Occasionally Killer stopped to sniff around. I could hear his nose running along the dirt, and the random doggie sneezes when he inhaled a big wad of dust. The tunnel twisted and turned through the ground. Once in a while I felt a breeze coming from a different direction, and had a sense of other tunnels branching off in other directions, but Killer seemed to know where he was going.

At one such intersection we paused for a long time. Killer seemed uncertain, tugging this way and that on the leash. Finally, in frustration, I decided to keep going. I could tell the way we'd been heading, and it seemed the right direction to me. Killer would catch up if I pulled on his leash I figured.

I went about two feet and walked straight into a wall.

*THUMP!*

"Ow!"

"Are you all right?" Frank was behind me and couldn't tell what had happened. I held my nose, trying to see if it was bleeding. I didn't think I'd broken it . . . but I wasn't sure.

"Joe!" Frank hissed.

"I'm fine," I said through the hands I'd cupped around my face. "I, uh, tripped."

Since he couldn't tell what happened, I saw no reason to let him know I'd actually walked directly into the wall. In a few seconds Killer picked up whatever scent he'd been following and took the lead again. This time, I stayed a few feet safely behind him.

In the dark it was hard to tell how far we had gone. Sometimes it felt like the tunnel was closing in around us, and I could almost feel the rough stone walls against my hand and the ceiling pressing down on my head. At other times it felt like we were walking through a giant empty room, and I wouldn't be able to touch the ceiling if I jumped. It gave me vertigo.

I started to wonder if Killer knew where he was going. For all I knew, he could be following the trail of some students who had last used this passage eighty years ago. Or the smell of a cat that had gotten trapped down here. It seemed likely that whoever had cut the hole in the floorboards had used this secret tunnel to do it without being noticed, but the map Frank had found had shown dozens of tunnels. How would we know if we were on the right track?

After what seemed like fifteen minutes, I was

about to suggest to Frank that we turn back—although I wasn't totally certain I knew which way "back" was. I opened my mouth, but Frank beat me to it.

"Do you hear that?" he whispered.

I cocked my head, but couldn't hear anything.

"No," I said. "I think we might be going the wrong way."

"I'm sure there's something up ahead," said Frank. "I can hear it, just barely. Let's just go a little farther."

We walked for another minute, and now I could hear it too. It was the sound of many people, singing at once. Or maybe not singing. Maybe they were chanting. The hairs on the back of my neck stood up. In the dark, with the voices echoing off the tunnel walls, it was impossible to tell if I was hearing two people or two hundred.

Killer's behavior started to change. He'd slowed down a lot. I could hear him sniffing the air. Soon I could smell it too—there was a fire somewhere up ahead. He was trained well enough not to make any noise, but I could tell that the smell of the fire had his senses on edge.

It began to get brighter. There was a flickering light coming from somewhere up ahead. Frank, Killer and I slowed down to a crawl. The voices were getting louder and louder. Whatever language they were chanting in wasn't English.

"Do you know what they're saying?" I whispered to Frank. He was always good with languages.

"No. But I'm pretty sure that it's Greek."

The mention of Greek triggered a thought, but it took me a moment to chase it down.

"ATAC said Erebus was a Greek god associated with death!" I hissed.

"Yep," Frank said, nodding. "And I think we're about to meet some friends of his."

The tunnel we were in ended in an abrupt turn, which led to a rough archway. The light and voices were all coming from beyond it. I crept up to the corner of the archway, knelt down, and peeked around the corner.

The room was large and circular, with four different entrances and a series of rough wooden torches along the walls. Standing in a circle were a dozen or so people wearing black robes and blank, white masks. They were all chanting together. I caught the word Erebus a few times, but the rest, as the saying goes, was Greek to me.

One of the robed figures stepped forward into the center of the circle. The other ones grew quiet. He seemed to be the leader.

"Tonight," he said. "One of our newest initiates

has brought great honor upon the Brothers of Erebus. By his deeds we know him to be truly worthy of membership here. He has proven himself."

As one, all of the other figures repeated "He has proven himself."

"By his courageous acts, we know him to be a true Brother of Erebus!"

The voice of the lead figure was familiar, but with the weird echoes in the room, and the way the mask muffled his words, I couldn't tell who it was for certain. But one thing I did know—the great honor brought to them tonight? They must have been talking about whoever had nearly killed Mill. This was some kind of death cult!

I tried to move closer, but the smoke and the fire from the torches aggravated Killer. He pulled back against his leash and whimpered. It was a quiet sound, but by some trick of the tunnel, it echoed into the chamber. Instantly, the masked figures whirled to look at the gateway where we were hidden.

"Intruders!" yelled the leader. This time I recognized the voice. Spencer.

*There goes that whole stealth approach,* I thought, as Frank and I both tried to get past Killer and through the door at the same time.

The cultists must have been trained on what to

do if someone discovered them, because the robed figures wasted no time. Each of them ran straight for the wall, grabbed a torch, and extinguished it. By the time we'd made it into the chamber, the whole place had been plunged into darkness. I could hear running footsteps and the *whoosh* noise of the fabric of the robes rubbing against the walls, but I could see nothing.

The one good part about the darkness was that Killer sprang back into action immediately, leading the way. I felt someone slam into me in the dark, and was nearly knocked over. I felt the pull of the leash as Killer leaped forward, barking. He hit someone, and they screamed. I reached out to grab them, and got a handful of sleeve. They pulled away before I could tackle them.

"We've got to get one of them!" I yelled.

"On it!" Frank's voice came from across the room. If we didn't catch any of them, we'd have no proof, no way of telling who any of them were—aside from recognizing Spencer's voice, and what kind of proof was that? All he'd have to do is deny it, and it seemed like the rest of the cult was pretty much a follow-the-leader type of crew.

I ran forward, blindly, hoping I wouldn't slam straight into a wall again. At the speed I was going, I'd definitely break my nose this time. Luckily, Killer pulled me along behind him as he ran, dodging this way and that, through doorways and corridors. Sometimes I heard footsteps—in front of me, behind me, getting closer, retreating. It was confusing and terrifying. My heart was pounding in my ears. Finally, after what seemed like an hour of running, I heard someone right next to me!

"Gotcha!" I yelled, and leaped. I knocked them right off their feet and landed on top of them, pinning them to the ground.

"Ow! Joe! It's me, Frank."

"Sorry!" I tried to help Frank up, and Killer's leash slipped from my hand. I could hear the sound of his nails clicking against the bare stone floor as he ran off.

"Quick!" I said to Frank. "We've got to follow him!" If we lost Killer in these tunnels, we might never see him again.

I followed the sound of Killer's footsteps deeper into the maze of tunnels. They got fainter and fainter, and soon I couldn't hear them at all. Just the sounds of Frank and me running. *We've lost him,* I thought.

Suddenly loud barking sounded up ahead.

"Help! Get him off me! Help!"

Looks like Killer had done our work for us! I ran toward the noise.

"Get him off!" It was Spencer. By the time we reached them, Killer had pinned the leader of the group! Good dog!

"Stay where you are!" Frank yelled. I got a firm hold on Spencer's wrist, then reached down to pull Killer off of him. I heard Frank rummaging around at my feet. There was a sharp sound of something metal being struck against the rock. Then a spark leaped out and lit the torch Frank had taken from Spencer.

I handed Killer's leash to Frank, reached out, and pulled off Spencer's mask.

We'd pretty much known that Spencer Thane was involved with the Brothers of Erebus. We'd already found out he knew about the tunnels, and Frank had found a torch in his room. Just about the only thing we didn't know was that he was willing to hurt—and maybe even kill—other students for this mysterious cult.

"All right," I said. "The game's up Spencer. We're on to you. Now tell us the truth. Why did you do it?"

"What are you talking about?" Spencer looked from me to Frank and back. "Why did I do what?"

"Mill! Why did you try to kill Mill? What is the Brothers of Erebus anyway?"

"WHAT?" His eyes grew wide. "What happened to Mill?"

I looked at Frank, and he gave me a tiny nod. It sounded like Spencer was honestly surprised.

"The floor—it collapsed beneath him during the show. Right near where your little secret door was hidden."

"I don't know anything about that. Really! All of us left before the concert started, to get ready for the ritual tonight. I wouldn't hurt Mill! You can ask any of the guys who were down here, we left early."

"Then what 'great deed' were you talking about?" said Frank. "Who were you letting into the Brothers of Erebus?"

Killer stepped forward and started growling while Frank was talking. He knew how to make people talk! Spencer flinched.

"Lee! I was talking about Lee. I'd heard he was going to win the Firth Spirit Award, and I knew that was the last thing I needed to convince the other members of the brotherhood to let him in. Most of our members are legacies, so I had to work to convince them to let him join."

"So you guys had nothing to do with the accident?" I let Killer's leash out a bit.

Spencer shook his head furiously.

"And you haven't been harassing Destiny? You didn't use one of these torches to burn that figure of her on the soccer field?"

"No! I mean, some of the guys pulled some pranks on her early on, but I knew Dr. Darity was already angry at GTT, so I made them stop. Besides, she probably did that herself—I mean, look what happened after she and Mill broke up."

I paused. This was the second time someone had blamed Destiny herself for the incidents. Suddenly, a number of signs were pointing back at Destiny. I was beginning to get suspicious.

"What are you talking about?"

"After she and Mill broke up! She faked all of these e-mails from him, and sent them around campus making it look like he had been harassing her. When people found out they were fake, she tried to pretend it was a joke, but everyone knows she's a total mental case! She blamed Mill for slashing her tires too, and there was never any proof of that either. If someone went after Mill, I'd look at her!"

Something clicked in my brain. Who could be close enough to Destiny to mess with the stuff in her bag? Destiny herself.

Who was in the theater all day helping set up,

giving them a chance to saw through the boards? Destiny.

Who smelled of smoke the day of the fire? Destiny.

Who would know about the private blood supply? Destiny.

Who had said she was going to "get back" at Mill herself? Destiny.

Who hasn't been concerned about her safety this whole time? Destiny.

All this time, our main victim should really have been our main suspect!

FRANK

14

## Secrets Revealed

With Spencer leading the way, we headed out of the tunnels. Joe and I were silent the entire way, stunned. All this time, Destiny had had us fooled. I wondered if she'd been responsible for all the things Ellery hadn't done—tampering with Lee's grades, the graffiti at Dr. Montgomery's house, the injured swim coach.

How far would she go for attention? What would she do next?

In my head, it didn't all add up. Sure, I could see why she'd harass herself for some attention, but what about the rest of it? Then again, she may just have been crazy, and lashing out at all the people she thought had been to blame for the hard time she'd been having at the Firth Academy. She seemed to have enough anger to pull something like that.

Finally we found a set of steps that led up into the hut out in the woods. Mr. Marks' bodyguard must have been surprised to see Joe and me accompanying Spencer out of the hut, but he didn't say anything.

"Can I go home?" Spencer asked once we were outside. "I have a test next week, and I really need to study." I'd almost forgotten, amid all this, that he was just a student. A kid, not used to dealing with this stuff like Frank and me.

"You can go," I told him. "But we'll want a full list of the people who were down in that room with you."

For a second, Spencer looked liked he was going to protest. Then he thought better of it.

"Ellery said something about you guys being spies, but I just thought he was making it up. He was telling the truth though, wasn't he?"

Neither Joe nor I said anything. After a moment Spencer left us and walked off toward the dorm.

"Well," I said, "there goes yet another person who knows we work for ATAC. Maybe we should take out an ad in the school paper?"

"No need. We can just announce it over the

loudspeaker during the game tomorrow."

That was right—the game was tomorrow. We needed to talk to Dr. Darity, and get Destiny taken somewhere safe. Who knows what sort of disaster she had planned for the game.

The Darity house was on the other side of campus from the shack in the woods. We headed there as quickly as we could. The campus was dead quiet. Everyone must have gone to bed early after the "accident." But as we walked across the main quad, I noticed the light was still on in Dr. Darity's office. Looked like he was working late. Somehow I wasn't surprised.

We went up to his office. I knocked on the door.

"Come in," said Dr. Darity, his voice both tired and surprised. He groaned when he saw us. "Let me guess—more bad news?"

Joe and I stared at each other. This wasn't going to be easy. It was obvious how much Dr. Darity loved Destiny. Starting with what Spencer had told us, we laid out the case for Destiny being the mastermind behind the incidents.

At first Dr. Darity didn't believe us. "All you have is the word of a bunch of kids," he said. "That's not proof."

I pulled the scrunchie from my pocket. "We

also found this beneath the stage, right by the saw that was used to cut through the floorboards. It's Destiny's. We have ATAC running the blood spot through their system. Once we have a match, it'll be too late for Destiny to come clean about everything. If she admits to it now, we might be able to get her some help."

It was pretty clear to me that Destiny had some mental issues. She didn't need jail—she needed to be looked after.

"She's a good girl," said Dr. Darity, mostly to himself. "It's just . . . these past few years have been so hard. She's been acting out ever since her mother died. But I never thought she would do something like this. . . . Millhouse could have died. The doctors said a few inches to the left, and one of those boards would have punctured his arteries."

Dr. Darity stood up and rubbed his eyes. He looked sad, but determined. "If we confront her now, is it ok if I keep her on campus until the end of the weekend? I'd like to avoid embarrassing her in front of her old school, as well as her new one. I promise I'll keep her under lock and key."

"So long as you can make sure she doesn't cause any more trouble, I think that will be okay," said Joe. He still had a soft spot for Destiny.

We assured him that ATAC would him find a place where she could go for treatment, somewhere quiet.

"All right boys. Let's do this now."

With Dr. Darity leading the way, and Killer pulling up the rear, we headed over to the Darity house. The light was on in Destiny's room when we got there.

Dr. Darity approached the front door of the house, then paused. "Frank—perhaps you should wait out here. Destiny has a history of climbing out her window when she doesn't want to talk to me."

"I'll intercept her if she does." I positioned myself on the ground, near the tree that was outside her window. If she came this way, she wasn't getting past me.

Dr. Darity and Joe headed inside. Sure enough, two seconds after the front door closed, Destiny's window flew open. First one leg made it through, then a second. Then a person dropped to the tree branch below and began climbing down to the ground.

But it wasn't Destiny. Not unless she'd cut her hair short, dyed it blond, and become a guy. It was Lee!

He made it all the way to the ground, and I

grabbed his arm before he could take off running. He yelled in surprise when I touched him.

"What are you doing here?" I asked.

"Me! What are *you* doing here? Look, man, I've got to get out of here before Dr. Darity catches me."

There was yelling coming from upstairs, but I couldn't make out what Destiny was saying.

"Oh man. I hope Dr. D. didn't see me. I'm going to be in so much trouble."

"More than you think," I muttered under my breath. I didn't know what he was doing here, or if he was involved with any of this, but I wasn't letting him out of my sight until we had some answers. It seemed like Destiny wasn't going anywhere, so I decided to head inside.

"Come on," I said, and pulled Lee toward the front door of the house. He protested for a moment longer, but then Destiny started yelling again. He stared up at her window with a worried expression. Then he sighed and started walking along with me.

When we got into the room, everyone stopped talking for a second. Dr. Darity cut off mid-sentence when he saw Lee.

"I know about the lies you've been telling and—Lee! What are you doing here?" Everyone in the room turned to look at Lee and me. Destiny turned bright red.

"Is this what you're talking about?" Destiny said. "Fine! Yes, I've been lying to you. I didn't want you to know Lee and I were dating. There! Are you happy now?"

"What?" Dr. Darity stared at Lee.

Now it was Lee's turn to go red. "I'm sorry Dr. Darity! I wanted to tell you sooner, but Destiny said not to!"

"But why wouldn't you tell me?" Dr. Darity turned to Destiny.

"Because he's just so perfect, and I didn't want you getting all excited to have me dating your 'Golden Boy.'"

"Hey," Joe broke in on them. "I'm happy for both of you, really—but that's not why we're here."

Everyone turned to look at him. For the first time, I noticed that Joe was pretty red in the face too. I was also pretty sure I hadn't imagined the edge to his voice as he said "I'm happy for both of you." Destiny *had* been flirting with Joe since we'd arrived on campus . . .

"What are you doing here, anyway?" asked Destiny. "This is the second time you've burst into my room for no reason."

"We know you've been the one behind all of

the pranks that have been happening, Destiny. We know you sawed through the floorboards on the stage, and set fire to that dummy of you. What we want to know is, why?"

Destiny laughed out loud. "What are you talking about?"

"Destiny . . . you can tell us the truth," Dr. Darity chimed in.

"Dad—you believe this stuff?"

Together, Dr. Darity, Joe, and I laid out the case against her.

At first, Destiny laughed—but then she realized we were serious.

"Look I faked those e-mails, sure. I was mad at Mill! And I didn't want to make my relationship with Lee public knowledge so I had to find *some* way to make him jealous." Destiny shot Joe a brief, apologetic smile before her expression turned serious again. "But I haven't done any of the rest of this stuff, I swear."

"You've lied before Destiny," said Joe, still clearly irritated by the fake flirtation. "How can we trust you now?"

"Because she's telling the truth," Lee piped up from the corner. "She couldn't have done that stuff with the blood, or set fire to that mannequin."

"How do you know?" I asked.

"Because I was with her that night. I met up with her at the bonfire. We hung out talking all night. And I was here when you guys burst in and thought she was dead."

Destiny nodded. "He was hiding under the bed. He didn't have time to get out the window, so he jumped under there when you guys came in the front door. That's why I was lying on the floor—I was trying to make it so you couldn't see him."

"She's innocent, I swear," said Lee. He walked over and put his arm around her shoulders. She smiled at him.

Now I didn't know what to think. All the evidence seemed to point toward Destiny. But if she had an alibi . . . could she be responsible for some of the pranks, but not all of them? Even with what Lee had said, she still could have dosed the papers in her bag with capsicum and booby trapped the stage.

Suddenly a beeping noise came from my pocket. JuDGE was finished analyzing the blood sample from the scrunchie! Now we'd know for sure.

I pulled JuDGE out of my pocket. "This should let us know who's telling the truth," I said. "We had headquarters analyze the blood on the scrunchie we found. Since they've been able to match your blood to your medical records before, Destiny, this will tell us if you've been lying. You sure you've told us the whole truth?"

"Yes!" said Destiny.

I flipped open JuDGE's screen. *SAMPLE UNIDENTIFIABLE.*

"Wow. I guess you were telling the truth." Joe let out a low whistle. Someone had been trying to set Destiny up!

Destiny smiled. "Ha! See, I told you so. Now why don't you go and catch the real creeps who've been doing this and leave me alone."

If Destiny wasn't the culprit, that meant she was still in danger. And since most of the threats had to do with soccer, it didn't take Sherlock Holmes to figure out that her attacker was going to try again— probably at or before the big game tomorrow. If we were going to stop them, we'd need Destiny on our side.

"I'm sorry we accused you Destiny. But if we're going to catch them, we need your help."

"What do you need me for?" said Destiny. She was still angry—but I could tell she was also flattered that we needed her.

"These pranks have been escalating. And the threats in your bag said they wanted you out of the big game. Which means they're probably going to try again."

Joe broke in. "So our best bet of keeping you safe—and catching this creep—is to let you go about the day as normal, but with Frank, Killer, and I keeping a close eye on you for when he or she makes their move."

"Absolutely not," said Dr. Darity. "A student nearly died tonight! I'm not letting this maniac have another shot at my daughter. Destiny, you're going to have to sit out the game."

"No way! I am playing in that game tomorrow. Joe—I'm in. Tell me what we need to do."

"Dr. Darity," I said. "Chances are whoever is doing this is going to keep after Destiny, even if you pull her out of the game. The only way to make her safe is to catch this guy and put him behind bars."

"I promise I'll keep an eye on her during the game too," said Lee. Destiny squeezed his shoulder in thanks.

Dr. Darity didn't like it, but eventually the four of us were able to convince him that it was the only way to make Destiny—and the Willis Firth Academy—safe in the long run.

"Okay," I said. "Then here is the plan . . ."

## Big Game

**W**e spent half the night devising our plan for the next day. We even woke up Spencer to get some more information about the tunnels. Then we took turns watching over the Darity house, to make sure nothing happened in the night. I took the first shift. By the time I finally returned to my cabin, Killer in tow, I felt like I was going to collapse. It was hard to believe it was all the same day: the dinner, the awards, Mill's injury, the tunnels . . .

It felt like I had barely closed my eyes before the sun was rising again, and it was time to get up and take Killer out. Then it was off to the soccer field.

Frank was already waiting for me when I got

there. The sun was just above the horizon, burning the dew off of the field. No one else was around. Together the three of us took a long walk around the soccer field, checking to make sure nothing had been tampered with, that there were no more mysterious trucks that could come flying down at a moment's notice, no sawed-through posts on the goal. So far everything looked normal.

The plan was pretty simple. Frank's map had indicated that one of the secret tunnels led to the building that Destiny was currently using as her locker room. We got Spencer to show us where the tunnel opened up in the house, and how to get to it. Because the house was so far away from the rest of the soccer field, we figured if anyone was going to come for Destiny, they would do it when she was in there, alone.

Frank was going to stake out the tunnel underground, to prevent anyone from getting in that way. We'd already shown Destiny how to get into the tunnel from inside the house, so if she needed it for a quick escape, she'd know where to go. Killer and I were going to hide among the bushes and stake out the house from the outside. Frank and I would use walkie-talkies to keep in constant contact. No one was going to get past us.

Once we were certain that everything was in order, I went back to the Darity house to escort Destiny to the field. Frank made his way to one of the underground tunnels, so he could guard the entrance in case one of the Brothers of Erebus was behind the attacks on Destiny. By this point, people were up and awake all around campus. We could already hear people cheering over by the soccer field, as one by one the various players showed up and began to stretch and warm up.

"Gee, thanks," said Destiny, as I held the door open for her.

"Hi Destiny." I scanned the sides of the house briefly, just to make sure no one was hiding there.

"You could act a little less like you're escorting me to my funeral, you know? This is, like, the biggest game of my life!"

"I'm sorry. Congratulations. I mean, good luck? Break a leg?"

She laughed and punched me on the shoulder. With Killer leading the way we headed over toward the field. Once Destiny had unlocked the door and was safely in the house that served as her changing room, I breathed a sigh of relief. I'd still been slightly worried that Destiny might have run off in the middle of the night, or that she would disappear at the last moment. I took up a position off the path, hidden among the trees, with Killer at my feet.

"Everything okay down there? Over." I spoke quietly into the walkie-talkie.

"Yup," said Frank. "Quiet as a grave down here. Over."

Now it was just a waiting game. I felt certain that our culprit was going to stage an attack on Destiny right here, right now. They had no other chance if they wanted to stop her from playing in the game.

For a few minutes nothing happened. Maybe we'd been wrong. Maybe the person had gotten scared off when they'd nearly killed Mill.

The sound of Killer whining broke in on my thoughts.

"What is it boy?" I looked around, but could see nothing that might upset him. Then I smelled it. Smoke!

I looked over, and the house looked the same. At least the outside did. But a thin trickle of smoke was coming from one of the front windows, and I knew that somewhere inside, a fire had been started. From the position of the smoke, it seemed like the fire had been started right in front of the main door! I ran to try to open it, but the door-knob was too hot to touch. How had someone gotten inside without us noticing? I broke one of the windows, and flames leaped out at me. This was the only real exit to the house—if Destiny hadn't known about the secret tunnel, she would have been trapped!

"Frank!" I yelled into the walkie-talkie. "We've got a fire! And I can't get in!"

### Frank

Frank here. Thankfully I was waiting for Destiny down below. She must have smelled the fire, because before I even made it to the entrance of the tunnel, she came flying down! I slammed the door behind her and barricaded it closed with some wood we had assembled down here for just that reason.

Destiny collapsed in a coughing fit behind me. After a few seconds she was able to catch her breath. "I was in the shower when I heard someone behind me. I turned off the water, and that's when I smelled the smoke."

Destiny had inhaled a lot of smoke, and I had to help her to the other end of the tunnel. Suddenly, someone slammed into the door and pounded on it for a minute, then stopped.

I radioed up to Joe. "They're still inside the house!"

**Joe**

Not to worry though. I had it all in hand top-side.

Like I was saying—I tried to get in the front, but I couldn't. That's when Frank hit me up on the walkie-talkie. I backed off and began circling the house with Killer. Sure enough, a minute later, someone was trying to crawl out of one of the upstairs windows. I waited until they'd leaped to the ground, then released Killer. They made it all of about two feet before Killer had them pinned.

Frank and Destiny came up behind me right as the culprit started screaming. "Get this dog off of me! Help!"

Destiny flinched when she heard the voice. "Casey?"

Two seconds later Casey no longer needed to worry about Killer hurting him—because Destiny had shoved Killer out of the way, and was busy kicking Casey into the ground. Frank had to wrestle her off of him, while I pinned him down to stop him from running away. Finally we got them separated.

"You were my friend! You jerk! Why would you do this?"

"You ruined my life!" screamed Casey.

"What are you talking about? I didn't even know you before you transferred here."

"Yeah, but you knew Lydia—remember her?"

"Lydia? From the soccer team? What about her?"

"You made her miserable for years. You shaved her head! She quit school after that, because she was too embarrassed to come back! She was my girlfriend. You ruined her life, and you ruined my life, and then you come here and you play against our team. Someone had to stop you from hurting more people!"

Destiny looked like she was about to run over and kick Casey in the face again. "Lydia smashed my computer! She stole stuff from me all the time. She made my life miserable too! She got what she deserved."

There was no point in letting this go any further. I broke in on the two of them.

"Destiny—the game's about to start. You need to get over to the field!"

For a moment Destiny looked as though she'd forgotten all about the game. Then, with a last evil look at Casey, she went sprinting to the soccer field. I looked at Casey. *Of course it was Casey,* I thought—he was close to Destiny so he could hide the things in her bag, he was also new to Firth

Academy and would have needed a map of the campus, and he had ample opportunity to steal her scrunchie and plant it at the scene of the crime. He must have stolen the key to the changing house from Destiny, and been waiting overnight for her to come in.

While Frank called Dr. Darity, I got a full confession from Casey. There were a few things he said he didn't do—the graffiti with her blood, the truck that nearly squashed her—but for the most part, he owned up to everything. Casey said he was sorry that Mill got hurt, but if Destiny had just dropped out of the game earlier, he wouldn't have been forced to go to such extreme measures. It was all her fault, Casey kept repeating.

To think all of this and to still pretend to be her friend . . . Casey must have been really messed up in the head.

Thankfully Dr. Darity and the police arrived soon. When we explained everything that had happened, they took him away almost immediately.

"Thank you boys," said Dr. Darity. "This makes twice now that you've saved my school—and once that you've saved my family. I don't know how I could repay you."

"All in a day's work, Dr. D.," I said.

"Just doing our job," chimed in Frank. "Now

let's go watch Destiny kick some butt on the soccer field!"

We headed over to the field together, Killer tugging on his leash. Finally this case was over and we could relax. Once the big game was done, we'd pack up our stuff and head back home. Which meant back to school for me, which I was trying not to think about—at least I'd be eating homemade food again. The cafeteria here was getting a little old.

By the time we got to the game, there was no question which team was going to win. Firth was running the field. The Blair team hadn't been able to score a single goal on Destiny. Lee had scored two of the three points that Firth had on the board. As we watched, a fast moving Blair player tried to sneak the ball up the inside through the Firth defenses. They made it right up next to the goal. They kicked—and Destiny just seemed to be there. She moved so fast I didn't even see her run. One second she was at the other end of the goal, the next, she was blocking the ball with her chest. Her team got it on the rebound, and Lee drove it straight up the middle of the field and into the opposite goal. It was now four to nothing, Firth.

In the cheering and whooping and shouting that

followed the big win, everyone seemed to have forgotten the terrible events of the last few weeks. For once people seemed happy and calm on the Firth campus. They'd even left behind the rivalry that had kept them from embracing Destiny as one of their own. The team lifted her and Lee up on their shoulders and chanted their names. Being the MVPs had its perks.

The winner's cup—a giant, two-handled silver vessel—was brought over. It was a tradition that the best player of the game drank punch from the cup. They tried to give it to Lee, but he shook his head and pointed at Destiny. They tried to give it to her, but she just pointed back at Lee. Everyone laughed, and finally someone from the crowd shouted that they should just share it. The two groups of students who were holding Lee and Destiny up brought them closer together, and, holding hands, they both drank deeply from the cup.

The crowd went wild. Even the Blair team cheered their opponents. Destiny must have spotted her Dad standing over with us, because she waved for the students to put her down. She began running over this way.

But something was wrong. She was running funny, sort of sideways, like she couldn't keep her balance. She opened her mouth to yell—and she collapsed to the ground. People started to scream. I looked behind her just in time to see Lee swaying in place where the students had put him down. Suddenly he collapsed as well!

I took off running toward Destiny and Lee, with Frank and Dr. Darity right behind me. I only hoped we weren't too late already.

# MORE TOTALLY TERRIFYING TALES FROM AWARD-WINNING AUTHOR

# JAMES HOWE